UNTIL THEN THERE'S COFFEE

every coffee has a story, a decision, a longing and a hope

Inkfeathers Publishing

Until Then There's Coffee
Edited & Compiled by Saranya Dhandapani
Print Edition

First Published Worldwide in 2021
By Inkfeathers Publishing, New Delhi, 110095

ISBN 978-81-948219-4-6

www.inkfeathers.com

UNTIL THEN THERE'S COFFEE

every coffee has a story, a decision, a longing and a hope

Edited & Compiled By

Saranya Dhandapani

Inkfeathers Publishing

DISCLAIMER

The anthology "Until Then There's Coffee" is a collection of stories by 21 authors who belong to different parts of the globe. The anthology editor and the publisher have edited the content provided by the co-authors to enhance the experience for readers and make it free of plagiarism as much as possible. All the stories published in this anthology are a work of fiction. Unless otherwise indicated, all the names, characters, objects, businesses, places, events, incidents- whether physical/non-physical, real/unreal, tangible/ intangible in whatsoever description used in this book are either the product of the author's imagination or used in a fictitious manner. Any resemblance to actual persons, objects, entities, living or dead, or actual events is purely coincidental. The stories published in this book are solely owned by their respective authors and are no way intended to hurt anyone's religious, political, spiritual, brand, personal or fanatic beliefs and/or faith, whatsoever.

In case, any sort of plagiarism is detected in the stories within this anthology or in case of any complaints or grievances or objections, neither the anthology editor, nor the publisher are to be held responsible for any such claims. The author(s) who holds the rights to the particular story, shall be held responsible, whatsoever.

CO-AUTHORED BY

Sara Elliott ~ Ida Williams ~ Padmini Peteri ~ Saranya Dhandapani ~ Harshita Garrepalli ~ Jaya Prakash A ~ Shaymi Shah ~ Karan E ~ Arati Harikumar ~ Anshika Prem Chhatani ~ Krupa Prakruthi ~ Dr. Deepiga R ~ Selvakumar Petchimuthu ~ Padmashri Jayaprakash ~ Archana Natarajan ~ Dheepan Ravikumar ~ Karthick A ~ Peter Jewkes ~ Prerna Agrawal ~ Suganya Kumar ~ C.L. Williams

CONTENTS

ABOUT THE EDITOR

Saranya Dhandapani

Saranya picked up her first cup of coffee when she was fifteen, but she picked up every other best thing in the world even before that. She learnt to enjoy music from her mother, she learnt to love from her father, she learnt to enjoy every little thing from her family. But those were just the seeds sown at the right time. She is still a coffee drinker, reader, and a passionate admirer of arts, but she is also much more than that.

Everyone who meets Saranya would have to pinch her hands to see if it's the reality because of the kindness which she showers on even the strangers who were fortunate enough to cross paths with her. She has a knack for nurturing people by gently nudging them towards progress, happiness, and achievement. She values and appreciates every little thing around her.

Not only that, she had led many professional meetings, work teams, and presentations which all had culminated as her latest but not last achievement of gathering and chasing a wild bunch of passionate writers towards their happiness, a published book.

It's easy for kindness to be taken as weakness, and love to be taken advantage of. But friends of Saranya know that is impossible with her. Not only as she is kind and gentle as a breeze, but she can also be a swirling hurricane or the burning magma that scorches the earth which is trying to hold it down. She is an indomitable force of nature whose kindness is one of choice but not out of options.

Just like any force of nature, she is also forgiving, beautiful, and complex. Yes, she is a coffee lover, writer, and anthology editor as of now, but she is and forever will be much more and much better.

EDITOR'S NOTE

Coffee has always been an integral part of my life. Ever since childhood, I have been listening to a lot of beautiful stories at my coffee time with my parents. Soon after, my reading and writing journey also demanded a cup of coffee. I can usually be found reading a book while drinking coffee or drinking coffee while reading a book. Ever since then, coffee has been my best companion. I firmly believe that every coffee has a story and a fond memory. I wanted to bring such coffee memories of people all over the world into a single book. That's how this book happened! The book is everything about how beautifully coffee has been turning our lives around.

The famous tagline "A lot can happen over coffee" always reminds me of every decision that I have made over coffee, everything that happened in my life over a cup of coffee. How many important decisions have we made while drinking coffee? How many books have we picked up to read while drinking coffee? How many times have we thought that coffee would make everything right? You know if you have a cup of coffee, you can handle anything in life. Have you met your love in a coffee shop? How many times have you both shared glances without knowing each other while drinking coffee? Do you have a favourite "Good Morning" Radio show which you cannot listen to without grabbing a cup of coffee for yourself? Do you have a separate playlist to listen over a coffee? With enough coffee, anything is possible. But how do you know how much coffee is enough coffee? We never knew it. But we can talk enough about coffee.

If you are an ardent coffee lover, you will end up having a lot of coffee while reading this book. Even if you are not a big fan of coffee, you might want to try one after reading the stories.

Thank you Amma and Appa for introducing me to the world of coffee!

Saranya Dhandapani,

Editor

1

THE STREETS OF SEVENTH AVENUE

by S.C. Elliott

How's your coffee?" Robin asked.

"I can tell you that it's quality," Alison replied.

"But" Metry interjected.

"I don't like it. It's too high brow for me." Alison pushed the glass aside and lit the end of her fat cigar. "Hopefully, this is better." She pulled on the Robusto until the end was lit like embers. The sweet but tangy smoke rolled out, a thick cloud that resembled a conversation bubble. Alison handed the cigar to Robin and reached for the neglected coffee. The bitter Cuban blend was more palatable paired with the after taste of the cigar.

Robin coughed a few times after her first drag. She passed the cigar back to Alison, her body jerking from the spasms. Metry smiled around his cigar. The pearly whites of his teeth vibrant next to the dried tobacco leaf. "Is that too high brow?"

Alison valiantly puffed on the Robusto. With the flick of her wrist, she presented it to Robin, who shook her head. She placed the cigar in the ashtray. "You live, and you learn," Alison stated confidently.

"Really, Confucius?"

"How would I have known otherwise?" Alison sipped at her coffee. The cigar had an overwhelming effect on her brain. It was buzzing. "I might have always wondered. Do I like cigars? Is Cuban coffee tasty? Now I know."

"Ours was really strong. You should try it Metry." Robin said before she tapped at her phone's screen.

Metry reached across the table and pulled the Robusto from its slot. "I guess I should. That way, I can try two hand-rolled cigars."

"How is your coffee?" Alison asked.

"It's awesome," Metry answered while he puffed out imperfect smoke rings.

"What did you order?" Robin projected, her head bent over her phone.

"An Americano. I've had it before."

"Maybe I should have ordered that," Alison suggested.

"You still can. The shop's open until 12:00AM."

Though it was 10:00PM, Ybor City was fairly inactive until 11:00. The city was like a cat; slumbering throughout the day, awaking in the evening to galivant. The streets of 7th Avenue were slowly amassing crowds of people gathered at their respective haunts.

"It's late. I don't think I want another coffee. I'll never get to sleep."

"Late. Can't you tell it's early by 7th Avenue standards?" Metry pointed across the street. The Club bouncer in all black was setting up rope along the sidewalk. Red drapes obscured the large windows.

"Well, I hope none of those people have to work at 8:00AM." Alison retorted.

"You're working the early shift tomorrow?"

"Yep. Bright and early. I'm pulling a double. Gabby called out the next few days. I guess she's sick."

"I'll see you at two." Robin looked up from her phone. "Sorry, Alex won't stop texting me." She dropped the phone into her purse.

"Yeah, me too. I'm scheduled the same." Metry supplied.

"You sure you don't want to party hardy, Alison? I could use the distraction." Robin reached for the still lit Robusto and hungrily pulled on it.

Alison looked down at herself. Tattered tank-top, frayed blue jeans, and tennis shoes. "Yeah, I'm sure. Just 'cause I don't go, doesn't mean you guys can't."

Robin's laugh was near hysterical. "Alex would freak if I went to the club alone with a guy."

"He should be worried. A charmer like me? I'm surprised he let you come for coffee." Metry sarcastically monologued.

"I don't think I'm really in the mood to party anyway. People watching is much better." Robin rose from her chair. "I do want another coffee, though. Ali, you sure?"

"I'm good on coffee," Alison answered.

"Metry? Another Americano?" Robin asked.

"You know it."

The street was alive with groups of people. Some standing outside bars, others sitting at patio tables on the sidewalks. Neon lights burned on every surface, advertising beers and every other vice. Kids that looked too young to have their own IDs lined up outside the club across the way. Their early arrival is more evidence of their inappropriate age than the acne that dotted one's face.

"To be young again." Alison comically inserted.

"Don't start. We are young. In fact, we're the best kind of young. We can do stuff legally while still getting carded." Metry stated.

"But one day they will be that young. We'll be older. No longer the best kind of young."

"That's true, but today is not that day." Metry looked over his shoulder at the kids who were turned away by the gargantuan bouncer and then he simply shook his head. "He really knows his stuff. I don't think he even ID'd them."

Alison laughed. "Would you need to? I suspect at some point you can tell just by looking." She paused and rubbed at her temples. "I'm not sure if it was the coffee or the cigar, but my brain is on fire."

"Probably the cigar. Does your head hurt?"

"No, I just feel weird. I wish I had a pen and paper." Alison reached for the beverage napkin. "Do you have a pen?" She inquired.

Metry made a show of looking in his pockets. His face was one of facetious surprise. "Where is my pen? I always keep in my pocket?!" He shook his head in false wonder. "I guess I don't have a pen."

"You're a jerk. You know that?" Alison grabbed her backpack from the ground and thoroughly searched it. When she found a marker, she brandished it for Metry to see. Dramatically she lifted her eyebrows in a repetitive motion to suggest success and ingenuity.

"What are you doing with the marker? Put that weapon down!"

"Nothing you need to be concerned about. I just have an incredible idea that I have to write down before I forget it." Alison stated.

The door to the Queen Cigar Bar and Café swung open. Robin returned to the table three coffees in tow. "Here we are." She sat them down on the wrought iron table. "Three Americanos. Sorry Ali, all for one and one for all."

"I'm actually glad you ignored my explicit answer," Alison replied. She reached for the mug and blew gently on the piping brew. After a timid sip, she sat the coffee back down and again called for the marker and napkin. She slowly scrolled onto it so as not to tear the thin paper.

"Really? Well, I'm glad. What caused this change of heart?"

"She has been inspired." Metry grabbed his own coffee but kept it between his hands, hoping to cool it down. "Thanks, Robin."

"Inspired. By what?" Robin asked.

"I don't know. All she told me is that she has an incredible idea and can't forget it."

"I hope it's not about my epic love life," Robin suggested.

Alison heartily laughed. "In the words of Cher, "As if."

"Uh. How dare you!" Robin shook her head in practiced bafflement. She reached for the forgotten glass of water and pretended to throw it in Alison's face.

Alison did not even look up. She continued to note on the now full square. She turned it over and repeated her process.

"Ever the drama queen, Robin." Metry pushed Alison on the shoulder to get her attention. Alison looked up, her face a mixture of question and exasperation. "What is the idea? You can't leave us hanging."

"Yeah, Ali, come on. Remember I'm actively seeking distractions." Robin added.

"It's an idea for a story."

"Yeah, we got that. What's the story about?" Metry wanted to know.

"It's about us." Alison handed the napkin over to Metry.

He cleared his throat, then began to read. "How's your coffee?"

2

THE COFFEE SHOP

by Ida Williams

It was raining. Bitter and cold the droplets hit the pavement, pooling into murky puddles. Eileen trudged along, coat zipped up to the chin and hair damp. Strands clung to the sides of her face like glue, and every so often a stray drop of water fell into the back of the coat, dripping down her neck. Everyone pushed through, heads turned down and umbrellas routinely colliding. It was all so dull and miserable. Thrusting her hands into the deep coat pockets, she waited at the traffic lights. Cars ran past, their headlights cutting through the downpour. One came a little closer than the rest and splashed a wave into the crowd. A unified grumbled moan rippled among them. She watched the traffic lights. Green. Green and still more green. There was not much point looking down at the wet patch she could feel spreading on the bottom of her dress. It was no doubt dirty and would need soaking later. It didn't seem to matter very much—just another lousy occurrence in an altogether lousy day. Finally, the colour changed, and with a slow shudder, the cars came to a stop. Eileen crossed the traffic, swept along by the crowd. The vehicles stood in a row, their windshield wipers swiping in unison from left to right. They almost looked alive, like a herd of cattle, engines purring ready to begin their stampede again.

It took her another five minutes and across two further streets before she reached her destination. Through the grey light of the overcast afternoon, she saw the yellow glow travelling down the pavement to meet her. The bell above the door jingled gently as she entered, and she was instantly engulfed by the welcoming aromas of freshly ground coffee and cinnamon. Spotting a free table in the corner, she moved her way through the warm room and chatter of voices and gratefully sank into the chair, giving a quick order at the bar on the way. Thank goodness there was a spot, it was always so busy. Pulling out her phone, she looked through her notifications. Nothing! Sighing, she leaned her elbows onto the table. She felt awful. Annoyed and miserable. It was no one's fault exactly, and loads of little things had been going wrong all day. The toast had burnt that morning, her favourite dress had caught and ripped on a door handle of all things, and the project at work had to be edited again. Yet more changes. She glanced down at the screen again. And of course, there was that. No reply. Still nothing.

"Paul, sit down now."

Drawn away from the phone by the raised voice, Eileen looked across to the table in front of her and at the curly-haired little boy glumly sitting back down on his chair. His mother continued her conversation undisturbed, "Anyway I told him that a gym membership would be such a waste of money. I mean he'll maybe use it for one day or two but, really, a whole year. It's wishful thinking. That's what it is."

"At least it's a healthy thought," replied her friend, sipping the coffee with both hands clutched around the small cup.

"But thoughts don't burn the calories. Although I can't complain too much. And I never do as you know." She adjusted her seat and perched on the edge of her chair. "Paul put down that spoon. I thought that I would redo the guest room in orange and pink." The woman tilted her head of curly red hair to one side as she spoke and rolled her eyes dramatically, "I'm so tired of the white and brown. I know. I know what you're thinking. I'm the minimalist girl, and it has been my thing. You remember how it was love at first sight."

From her table in the back, Eileen suppressed a smile and watched the two women chatter away, their concerns lifting her for a moment away from her own.

"But honestly, I am just craving a little clutter. Some more nick-knacks and things," the red-haired woman continued, shrugging, and motioning from side to side with her spoon. "I do feel rather bad about it . Like I'm cheating on a diet or something. Paul, don't play with the sugar."

The little boy set down the sugar cube he was balancing on the edge of his cup and folded his arms. "Mommy?"

"I'm thinking orange curtains and a pink trim around the door. Not bright pink or anything too garish but something elegant. Did I tell you about the little crochet lamas I saw online yesterday?"

"Mommy, can we go now?"

"They are the cutest things ever. I'll show you a pic, I'm always saving things like this. Oh, you know the room where these would go perfect in."

The little boy pulled on his mother's arm, but the lamas won as a phone was taken out of a handbag. He leaned back into the chair, defeated, and stared at the ceiling.

There was something in his expression, a sense of futility that made Eileen feel for him. Not everyone pays attention or listens, even when you grow up. Not even at work where you're being paid to do a job. To make decisions. Even then, people don't always listen to what you have to say. All they want are edits. For any particular reasons? No. Even if they don't make the project better. Of course. Why not. Just edit this super quick. Super quick... nothing was ever super quick. She breathed in and out. Well, perhaps it was not quite as bad as all that. She peeked down quickly at her message app once more. It remained blank. Maybe it was better that way. With luck, she had been having that day.

"Honey it's a wonderful idea."

Another female voice interrupted her thoughts. A young couple in the booth by the door was leaning forward into the middle of the table and gazing at each over a potted succulent. Sitting both on the same side had obviously not occurred to them.

"You're sure baby? I don't want to rush you or anything."

"Rush me!" The woman smiled and clasped his hand, "We are one hundred per cent ready for this." Her enthusiasm seemed to draw him further into the table like a magic spell.

He grinned back, and they held hands for a while. "I'll help you move in tomorrow."

"It's so exciting. Just think of you and me living together."

"When we're settled, I also thought that we could maybe, you know, if you wanted, get a cat perhaps."

"A cat!" she squeaked, "Oh yes. I love cats. We could get one of those cat trees."

Eileen rested her chin in the palm of a hand and tried to ignore the creeping fingers of loneliness. Why were some couples extra cuddly? And why were they always sitting near her? She looked away. Just another reminder of something she didn't have. Where was that coffee? Why was it taking so long?

There was a line of customers over by the bar, each one looking intently at their phones, swiping through the day's headlines and feeds. She looked down at her own phone sitting by her hand and resisting the urge to recheck her messages, she put it away into her coat pocket. Checking every two minutes wasn't helping anything anyway. How many hints did she have to drop? Maybe she should just ask him out. That would be so much simpler.

The sound of medieval chimes pulled her back once more into the room and away from all her drifting concerns.

A middle-aged man wearing a grey flannel suit sat against the wall, the table strewn with papers. He answered the call, the phone in a sturdy hand. "Hello. Yes, I've run the numbers. Yeah, it will work fine to extend the budget into the next quarter." He shifted through the pile in front of him and pulled out a small notebook from underneath. "We need to coordinate with sales and marketing to take advantage of the holiday rush, but the budget would be better spent then than before...Yes... I have a projection for that." Keeping the phone slightly away from his ear, he looked downward with a vacant expression on his face, speaking at intervals and occasionally making a note.

Eileen watched him rub his eyes, the grey bags heavy and protruding. Not everyone liked their jobs. Not everything was exciting.

Finally, the barista came over with a tray and a steaming cup of coffee. "Sorry for the wait. We're always busy on rainy days," she said cheerfully, placing the order down on the table. "It's nice and friendly in here. Enjoy your drink."

Picking up the cup, Eileen blew into the frothed milk. It was friendly there. It always was. Maybe that was why she had come out of her way using up precious minutes of her lunch break to walk through the rain. To be surrounded by a chatter of voices, a warm atmosphere, and a hot drink. Nothing was as lousy as it felt. As she took her first slip, she suddenly felt really foolish. There had been too much complaining in her own head that day. Things would happen in their own time. A much better job, a boyfriend, and a family. Everything when it was ready. She took another sip. Everything was fine. It really was. Actually, probably even better than just fine.

Raising her hand, she caught the eye of the barista at the bar and motioned for a second cup of coffee. The little boy had now fallen asleep, curled up on his chair whilst his mother had an extra moment with her friend. The couple had moved the potted plant to one side and were talking in whispers, and the man in the grey suit had pulled out a scruffy looking novel, his papers laid to one side.

Smiling, she leaned back in the chair and turned to look out the window. Outside, the rain was still thudding down, and the city lights were dancing in the puddles in an array of cheerful colours.

3

A CUPFUL OF SOUL

by Padmini Peteri

My mornings cannot start without exercise and coffee. I enjoy a cup of coffee with my parents. No matter how busy we are, having coffee together is a tradition in our family which I have enjoyed since my childhood. My mom jokes about how I would kick when I was in her belly whenever she had coffee.

Just when I had the first sip of my filter coffee, my dad said, "So what are your plans for today, Vyom?"

I smiled all excitedly and said, "Dad, do you remember my school friend Dheeraj? He is back in India, and we made plans to catch up on all the old days after ages."

"Wow, that is awesome news to kickstart the day!" Dad said.

We finished our coffee chatting and were enjoying nature like we do every other day.

I got dressed and glanced into the mirror wondering if Dheeraj would recognize me, because back in school I was a chubby boy, in fact, both of us went hand in hand being the chubby boys of the school. Only in my intermediate, I realised the importance of a healthy body and started working out and looking after my body like I should, and also gave up unhealthy food habits. Still, one thing I can never give up is coffee, because it is not just a drink; it is a memory I cherish with my loved ones.

I rushed to the coffee shop and waited excitedly for my friend Dheeraj. Usually, guys catch up at a bar or a restaurant. Still, I prefer a coffee shop, the soothing ambience, a perfect blend of coffee, roasted aromatic coffee beans, that refreshing, inducing smell just makes my day perfect.

I smiled to myself thinking how life has changed since I had the last cup of coffee with Dheeraj back in high school, and now after six years, I cannot wait to hear from him.

Just then a tall, skinny guy arrives with a smile as large as a 75 mm screen and punches my hand which obviously didn't hurt, but I did flinch. One look at him and all the long-lost emotions were back, how healthy, and chubby he was back in school, how skinny, and fragile he looks now, we gave that tight fist punch and sat down to talk about everything and nothing.

We checked out the menu, and I ordered an Inverted Filter Cappuccino with Jaggery and Dheeraj ordered a Devil's own. We opted for a Tandoori Chicken Sandwich.

"So, how's life?" I asked Dheeraj.

He smiled pleasantly and said, "Life has changed a lot. It has been challenging, but I'm doing a great job. Don't you think so Vyom?"

I smiled, reminding myself of how carefree, irresponsible he was back in school and how courageous he emerged out.

"So why don't you tell me about all the things we missed out on? It has been so long, but I still feel connected though we were in touch at times through mails, seeing face to face is a different feeling."

"Yes, it does," said Dheeraj. Just then our amazing coffees and sandwiches were served.

I sipped my coffee, and he licked the whipped cream off his devil's own, like a funny little boy.

He started with a faint smile, "you know Vyom, it was a tough time. Soon after 10th, I started falling sick, I felt fragile, poor appetite. Do you remember that I took admission in MPC but soon after I started attending college, I felt a pit in my whole body and there was a piercing pain in my joints, arms and legs. It was too tiring because we did not know what it was. That was the time I guess I could not stay in contact with friends as I usually did."

"Yeah! that was the time it all started" I whispered to myself.

Dheeraj continued, "Later when I went to the doctor and underwent a couple of examinations, blood tests, we got to know that it was leukemia, a type of cancer that affects the bone marrow. It was a tough fight, I would not have survived without the help of my family. But there came a time when my parents were too scared and gave up hope. They just could not watch me in pain. My brother and sister-in-law were unbreakable pillars, and the rest you know what happened I underwent treatment in the U.S. Health facilities in the U.S are pretty good but expensive. My brother gave up his job and looked after me from my morning cup of coffee and medicines to my last morsel of the day. Whereas my devoted Sister-in-law worked day and night trying to earn more than she could for my treatment and everything. Luckily, we had insurance facilities that did help a bit, but my family's support was incomparable. It took years to recover from the side effects of chemotherapy, of the disease itself and somewhere down the lane I also started getting anxiety attacks due to all the pain my body went through. I was bound to break down mentally too. And do you know Vyom, what helped me the most other than medicines?"

"I'm sure it was your family," I said, having the last sip of coffee.

"Family, medicines, a bit of therapy and a lot of Coffee. Though few doctors said caffeine is not suitable for people with anxiety, but in my situation, it helped ease the stress."

"Dheeraj, I can totally connect, how we used to have fun all-round the year and at the time of exams, coffee would help us stay awake and study late nights?"

"Oh yes, how could I forget those days Vyom? I wish we could go back to those carefree days."

"Well! Is your anxiety and everything else fine Dheeraj?" I said, praying at the back of my head to hear the words "All good!".

"I feel better now, no anxiety attacks and my health is ok, but I do have doctor appointments every other 6 months just to make sure all is well. After getting cured from cancer, I really could not let go of my brother, he was my support system, and I was not mentally ready to come back to India. So, my brother suggested that I stay there and continue studying. That is what I'm doing. I'll be back to the U.S after my vacation."

My heart ached to know the immense pain Dheeraj went through. I said "Bro! Do you know what I think of you now? To me, you are like the phoenix, who rose from its ashes. I'm so proud of you man" and punched his fist in a brotherly way. In those eyes, I could see how proud he felt of himself. He truly lived to the meaning of his name Dheeraj which means Courage.

"So Vyom enough of my story I want to know what is happening in your life?" Dheeraj asked.

I smiled and said "Well! Life is full of surprises when you found solace in your family's support, I found myself being softened like butter in someone's presence."

"Woah, bro! You softened in XYZ's presence is something unbelievable. I have always known you as a stormy person. What softened your heart?" Asked Dheeraj, pinching my cheek.

"Well, it is a long story," I said.

"Go ahead, we can order as many coffees as we want."

We ordered our second round of coffee.

I hesitated but smiled and started my story.

"There was this girl named Nirvi in college who loves to read, I never spoke to her because she seemed to be an introvert. I observed that she read when she was happy, read when sad, when anxious, when confused. It was evident that she dealt with her emotions by reading a book. Every day I would see her at college, there was a book in her hand, and at times she tripped over and fell because she was so engrossed in her book."

"What the hell bro how could she be so irresponsible? Reading a book when walking and tripping, I would be embarrassed. Wasn't she Vyom?" Said Dheeraj, impatiently.

"Well, I would be embarrassed too", I said sipping coffee, "but she was not."

"Trust me even when she tripped, she would not let her book fall, she was too busy protecting and hugged it like it was her beloved." That beautiful memory brought a smile on my face but was distracted when Dheeraj smirked saying, "What kind of a crazy bookworm is she?"

"Well! Do you want me to continue or should I chuck it, Dheeraj?"

"Oh no please, go ahead bro."

"Hmm, she would get up, dust her dress and continue reading, nothing mattered more than her books. Literally Nothing!" I stressed on that word because deep down, I wished that at least occasionally her gaze would transfer to the world outside.

"And you know what Dheeraj when classmates were waiting for a movie to be released, she was checking out new book releases."

"Wow! Really bro?" said Dheeraj.

"Nirvi was a mysterious girl who would not talk to many, but to her books, I guess she was less mysterious. I saw her smiling, blushing, in anger, in tears, when she read, she experienced a million emotions, it was so wonderful to watch her emotions being expressed like an open book like she was living in a book realm. That look on her face just soothed me. And I am sure Dheeraj, her best friends are characters from the book. I observed that she read a variety, from Fiction to Nonfiction, from Drama to Poetry, From Biographies to Autobiographies, and when she had nothing to read, can you guess what she read?"

"Umm, I don't know, well did she read her lecture notes or something Bro?"

"Seriously lecture notes? Did you have nothing else to think about Dheeraj? I have never seen her reading lecture notes, but she was in the top 3 of the class. Well, back to the track so when she had nothing to read, she read the dictionary or encyclopedia."

"What!!??" He said it out aloud, spitting some coffee out onto his cup.

"The more I watched her, I saw how blessed she was. Between her pages of the book, she found peace and comfort. She also made me realise that a person may betray, a relationship may cease to exist, but the bond we share with books remains, the bond she shared with reading was comforting to watch. It was like watching an angel bless a little baby. She was in her happy place because she had her books, it was evident that she found her peace in books. And I found my peace while watching her."

"Silent lover boy?" laughed Dheeraj.

I smiled and said, "Maybe! That smile she had on her face when she was with her books gave me an immense hope for something I desire in life, but I still did not know what it was. But at that moment all I wanted was to talk with her or get acquainted which seemed impossible. However, I made a conscious effort to speak to her, yet she was engrossed in her book realm. One day I went to a bookstore and decided to buy an amazing book for her, she had so many for sure, so I was not sure what she would not have. I checked many, and I decided on this book named Complete Works of Shakespeare with notes of characters or something after each play. I felt like I will play it safe and go ahead with a classic. The next day I went early to college and placed the book on her table with a little note inside.

It read: 'Hi, I love the way you adore books. Hope this classic brings more joy in your life. Happy reading!'

"Did you leave a note but not your name or number? Come on! that was one chance you had should have made use of it bro", said Dheeraj.

I smiled and continued my story.

"A week later, I placed another book on her table named IKIGAI with a note that had my number. And the next day I got a message from her thanking for the books. She said that IKIGAI was on her book list to read."

"Wow! so finally you exchanged numbers," exclaimed Dheeraj.

"Yes, and guess what? We will be getting married next year soon after she finishes her Masters."

Dheeraj was tongue-tied and could not speak a word.

Only after I pinched, he winced and said, "Bro, when did your love story even begin that you decided to get married."

"I think it is enough for today, we can discuss my beautiful love story the next time we meet over coffee. What say Dheeraj?"

Dheeraj was very surprised and said, "Until there's coffee, there will be more stories for us to catch up", and we waved each other goodbye.

4

ONE WORD FOUR LETTERS

by Saranya Dhandapani

There are two kinds of people: Those who write beautifully and those who enjoy such beautiful writings. I belong to the latter. I don't write, but I solve puzzles. I love Numbers. I don't fall for the idea of "Books, Coffee, Rain." My idea of a happy life is "Numbers, Puzzle, Math." Yes, I am a lover of Mathematics.

That was a September morning; the sun did not shine. It was not too wet or too dry, but it was cold, not all cold. When life gives you a "not so rainy day," solve puzzles. That day, I was struck with a puzzle, I terribly needed a coffee. Still, I couldn't solve it, so I decided to take a break from my puzzle and took a picture of my puzzle book and the Coffee. I wanted to post on Instagram with a good caption. I started searching for a caption in google. I came across a post that reads "Letters to Coffee." I followed the link, and it took me to a blog. There were more than 30 posts about Coffee. The writer's love towards the Coffee was insane, but I loved the metaphors and writings.

I was reading all the posts to get one caption for my photo. I saw a picture in one of the posts. The picture was taken on a terrace balcony, the background was full of tall, green trees, a phone, a pen, a red colour Bluetooth speaker, and a book "More Puzzles to you" by Shakuntala Devi, and a beautiful coffee mug. It's not the picture, but the caption. The caption was, "Sometimes, Mathematics is better than fantasies." That's what I was exactly looking for in the past 20 minutes. I started exploring the Blog again after posting the picture with the right caption on my Instagram.

Who is the writer? Is that a he or she? After 3 Hours, 18 Minutes, 59 Seconds of reading her blog, I saw a picture of her with 34 Coffee mugs in one of the posts. I found her wonderfully weird like "Phoebe" from "F.R.I.E.N.D.S." Her words are more beautiful than her. Also, she loves puzzles and math. Her father is a Maths Teacher, and it was him who started gifting her all the puzzle books. I got to know this from her "Happy Father's Day" post. I liked her words and her effortless skill of associating little things in her writing. I wanted to talk to her. I wanted her to solve the puzzles I give.

I wasn't doing anything from the morning except reading her Blog. I did all the micro search in google and found her Instagram profile, "The aficionado writes." That's her profile name. I gave a follow request, and She accepted right away. I didn't want to waste any time, and I texted her, "Hey... I read your Blog. I hardly took 46 minutes to find your Instagram profile. Also, I counted your coffee mugs in one of the pictures. Is it really 34 or more? I guess it would be more. I love F.R.I.E.N.D.S and Big Bang theory too. So How does it work? If you like any series, you will go and buy a customized coffee mug.... I am curious."

"Haha... Mostly! Yes! I am glad you loved my Blog (three "See No Evil" monkey emojis). I have more than 34 mugs. You are right!"

"I thought you'd not accept my follow request."

"I liked your bio 'to thine own self be true,'. So I accepted immediately!"

"Whoah! Hamlet is my favourite play, by the way. I love Shakespeare."

"Me too! What's your interest? Do you read? Where do you work?" She asked a lot of questions.

"Sanjana...are you taking an interview or what?!!! Save some questions for the future. L.O.L."

"Hahaha...Sorry! Don't worry, I will have more questions in the future also."

"I am Akash, Graphic designer. I love numbers, and I enjoy solving puzzles. Sometimes I read books. I can answer for you as well. Sanjana is a Software Engineer! Coffee Lover! She reads and writes a lot. If your bio is good, she will accept the follow request right away. She talks a lot. She asks a lot of questions. Any day sooner, she would own a Guinness record for having the highest number of Coffee mugs."

"I thought you are good at numbers, but you are good at stalking also."

"If I like 'like' you, I can guess your favourite number. If I guess the right number, we should go for a date. But you should be honest."

"Go ahead, Mr. Akash! But I will also ask you a question... The date is "ON" only if I am satisfied with your answer. Got it???"

"Yes! Ms. Sanjana! That's fine by me. Your favourite number is 7. Am I right?"

"WHAT!!!! HOW!!!! YES...... IT IS 7!!!!"

"That's one secret I would never tell! When I make a new friend, I give them a number in my head. I gave you 7, and it turned out to be your favourite number."

"Crazy!!! Now, it's my turn. Tell me your top five favourite movies. If 3 from your list matched with mine, it's a DATE."

"Easy, Peasy! Here I go- Her, Forrest Gump, The Reader, The Notebook, Eternal sunshine of the spotless mind."

"Why don't I believe you? Maybe you are good at stalking! I can't accept this answer because it's perfect."

"Nowhere in your Blog, you mentioned your favourite movies. That's my list! If it matches with yours, it's pure coincidence."

"Well! Maybe it's just a coincidence."

"You like solving puzzles, right? How about we meet over a cup of Coffee and give each other puzzles to solve?"

"Sounds perfect to me! I'm in!" She replied.

We were giving each other puzzles and solving them. Our puzzle marathon and the conversation continued for 10 hours straight. I couldn't stop myself from asking, "How much did you enjoy talking with me?"

"Infinity minus one."

"Why minus one?"

"Because plus one would make a lot of difference, doesn't it? I am sleepy already and tired of solving all your stupid puzzles. Will meet tomorrow at 99kms Coffee shop. You better sleep soon, else you wouldn't be able to solve the tough questions I have for you tomorrow. Bye Akash!! It was nice talking with you, or should I mention 'solving puzzles with you?!!' "

"I thought you would choose either C.C.D. or Starbucks. 99kms Coffee shop is an interesting choice seriously."

"You guessed my favourite number and movies. That's it! You'll get to know me more tomorrow."

"Fingers crossed," I replied and kept my phone away. The only thing I thought Sanjana would sleep with would be Books, notes, and her Coffee mugs. If anything, maybe a picture of Coffee. I'm grateful for deciding to have Coffee today. As she said in one of her writings, it's not about "How do we take our Coffee? It's about "Why do we take our Coffee?". Now I have the answer

Puzzles were always enough for me until I knew her. Right now, she is the puzzle I'm trying to solve. We spent the entire day chatting and asking silly yet different questions to each other. Every time she solved a puzzle, I felt like she changed my world like a butterfly flapping its wings. I challenged her answers, she challenged my questions. I gave her both solvable and alien puzzles; She gave me the right and the alien answers. I am a number without zero; she gave value to my numbers and to my craziness in solving puzzles. We were talking in ASCII code and binaries. We discovered a lot of permutation and combination theories. I started thinking about the probability of her having a crush on me. Sometimes it was infinity, other times it was just zero.

Meeting a girl and solving puzzles with her is my idea of an ideal date—the date which I thought would never happen. I thought she was just another "Procaffeinating queen." But she is not! She understands my craziness, and she is ready to jump into it. That conversation is the song I was playing in a loop. That's the conversation I always wanted next to my numbers.

I met her the next day! It wasn't like we were meeting for the first time! She reminded me of her writeups, simple yet complex. Each feature of hers hiding a different story. Her prettiness was epic and rich, just like the words she writes and the picture she captures. She was sitting right opposite to me, and I kept daydreaming about her, constructed fake dates with her, where she would recite her stories, and ask me how I found her favourite number.

"Are you a textrovert? Why are you so silent? Anna...Two filter Coffee, Strong," she said and looked at me.

"I think you got brain damage from solving too many puzzles too fast. I'm so excited to meet you and talk more about your superpower skills in Math. But you hardly talked since I came here, "she ended sadly.

"If you'd meet you now, you'd forget everything else and be silent too. I am trying to solve a puzzle from last night. I am not able to solve it. Not even closer!"

"Show me the puzzle! We will solve together!" her voice was so enthusiastic.

"You! You are the puzzle I am trying to solve. Numbers were always enough for me until we started talking. Let's solve this puzzle after getting you some of that Coffee you love so much".

She was puzzled. I figured out from her facial expression.

Our Coffees arrived. We started drinking slowly. I know our future will be just like us: flawed and fragmented and full of Sanjana's write-ups and my numbers and more of love than I ever thought possible.

"I came here to talk with you. But for the first time, words aren't enough for me, too" She sighed and started looking at her phone.

"I like you, Sanjana. I loved every single minute we spent together. Talking about your stories, discovering our own Math theories, solving puzzles. I enjoyed every bit of it. I like you- INFINITY PLUS ONE times than how much you like me. If I say I LOVE YOU and if you say it back, that will become a PALINDROME! Only if you say it back! That is all I needed now. I love you," I said. For a minute, our universe went silent.

She kept her coffee cup and started, "I want to tell you something."

"You've been telling this for the past 11 minutes."

"You were counting?"

"Every second... I can't help but want to hear it from you."

"Oh, Really??!!!"

"Come on, Sanjana...those 3 words, 8 letters have waited enough now!"

"Why are you so obsessed with numbers?"

"Why are you so obsessed with "not telling your feelings right away," don't tell me that's the reason you started writing."

"You got me!"

"This isn't the 3 words, 8 letters I was talking about."

"What do you want me to tell you now? Akash"

"4 words, 11 letters, do you love me?"

"1 word, 3 letters, yes!!! You know what? The definition of a 'happy day' changes with every happy day. I know you would make me happier in every tomorrow than every yesterday."

'The Aficionado writes started following you' my phone notification popped. I looked at her and asked in a very disappointed tone, "Sanjana...you didn't follow me yesterday??"

She didn't let me complete the sentence. "Yes, Akash! It took me 21 Hours, 19 Minutes, 27 Seconds to follow you back on Instagram" she came towards me and hugged.

That's it! That's my happily ever after.

Both of our Coffee had the same taste, the same heat until we finished drinking it! Pythagoras was right! Number rules the universe! In my benevolent circle of life, she is my Pi.

5

TWO SOULS, ONE COFFEE

by Harshita Garrepalli

On an evening, unlike no other, the usually quiet, muddy road on Avenue Street made noise. Two children were racing. One barely brisk walking, actually.

"I'm exhausted, Kyra. Can we please sit?"

"Advik, oh, Advik. You weakling. As you always have been."

Advik rolled his eyes.

"We have probably run like, five kilometers from our neighbourhood already. Weakling, you say?" he said.

"Whatever," Kyra said, pushing Advik, playfully.

"Can we go home now? Sun's almost down."

"It doesn't matter. I'm only going home on one condition."

Advik looked confused. After Kyra raised her eyebrows and over insinuated what she was talking about, Advik finally understood.

"Are you serious? I am sore in so many places, and you want me to carry you home?"

"No.... what? Why would I ask you to carry me home, I can walk, unlike you."

"Oh, thank god," Advik said, under his breath.

"Anyway, remember the bet? Where the loser of this marathon would cook something for the winner? Since we're both terrible at cooking?" Kyra said.

"Fine! I'll make something." Advik said.

As they began the walk home under the rosy skies, Advik told Kyra how he'd make a burnt vegetable stew and disguise it as chocolate cake.

***

The next morning, Advik awoke to the shrill screaming of a bird, instead of his alarm, only it wasn't a bird, it was Kyra.

"You demon! Let me sleep." Advik said, irritably.

"No time for that. Make me a meal, servant." Kyra mocked.

"I wouldn't want to be in a kingdom where you're the queen."

After fifteen minutes of childish banter, Advik finally went to the kitchen, still half asleep.

Soon after, he came out with a cup in his hand. Kyra was expecting breakfast, not just a plain beverage, so she voiced her argument.

"I thought you were going to get me something better than this." She said, pointing very passionately at a hot cup of coffee.

"Come on. I wasn't going to make you a five-star meal. This is my first-time making coffee. Try it and tell me if it's decent."

Kyra looked disappointed, but she picked up the hot cup of coffee. The invigorating smell of coffee beans filled the room. She took one whiff from the cup and was intoxicated. She closed her eyes and leaned back, resting her head on the chair.

Advik clapped his hands and Kyra snapped back to reality. "What are you doing? You didn't let me sleep, and here you are!" Advik said.

Kyra didn't respond, and immediately let the cup kiss her lips. One sip of the coffee was enough for her. She stared at Advik in disbelief. Had he really made this coffee?

Kyra put the cup down on the table and got up from her chair. "All right, where's auntie?" she said, frantically searching the kitchen.

"What? Oh! I get it. You don't believe that I made this coffee, do you?" Advik accused.

Kyra stopped and looked at an angry Advik with scared eyes.

"Well...obviously. I mean, you can't cook. You definitely could not have pulled this off." Kyra said.

"I could, and I did. My mother taught me a secret recipe for her special coffee, and for the record, she's out with your mother, jewellery shopping!" Advik said, disappointed.

"Oh! I'm sorry, Advik. This is phenomenal. It's nothing like what I've had on the Bengaluru Railway Station before. I'm genuinely impressed." Kyra apologised.

"Thanks...? Is this a dream? Is your highness complimenting the servant? For the first time ever?" Advik smiled.

"Yes. Now massage my feet."

"Ew, no. They smell."

The troublesome honking of a car jolted Kyra awake. After she failed to ignore it, she got out of bed, begrudgingly, and went outside. What she saw completely drove out her drowsiness. Suitcases; lots of them, packers and movers, big trucks, all in front of Advik's house. Kyra knew what was happening, but she hoped to God it wasn't true. Advik couldn't be leaving.

She ran over to his house. Advik's mother was there, carrying two bags containing steel boxes stacked on top of each other, buckled in with a steel belt, filled with food.

"Auntie!" she yelled, running to his mother.

"Kyra," Preeti said, in a tired voice.

"What are all these bags for?"

Preeti put down the bags and exhaled. She wiped the sweat off her face with her dupatta.

"Raj's gotten an immediate transfer to Mumbai. He got a promotion, but it came with a price."

Kyra's world came crashing down. Her best friend since day one, the only person whose opinions ever mattered, she would lose it all.

She stood, frozen in place, as "Paradise Packers & Movers" moved more cardboard boxes into the truck.

Advik was shuffling through every last thing he could find in his closet when he heard the echo of footsteps in the empty house and turned around.

Kyra was there, with tears in her eyes.

"Hey-"

Kyra slapped Advik with all the power she had. He covered his left cheek with an astonished look. "Ow! What was that for?"

"Yesterday, when we were playing Halo, everything was fine! You didn't tell me you were leaving. We were drinking your brilliant coffee. Oh, god! It's just been a while since I've finished drinking that coffee. Ugh, no! I'm going to miss it."

"Stop spiralling!" Advik interrupted. "I know it seems all sudden because it is! I didn't know until after you left last night that my father got the transfer and we had to move out so quickly. I'm sorry."

"What? That's merely unfair! You didn't care to come over and deliver this news to me? I'm disappointed, Advik."

"I thought your mother might've told you! She knows. I was going to, but I was wallowing in my own misery, okay? I didn't feel like telling anyone. I was so frustrated and angry."

"I can't believe this! Ugh, If I'd gotten to know such bad news, I would've told you first."

"You don't know how I was feeling at that moment, all right? I love you, but I'm just sick and tired of you thinking that you can boss me around." Advik said.

Kyra's eyes froze at Advik. Her lips pursed.

"Well, I'm tired of having to carry around a weakling like you. Always crying, being boring, I could go on all day." Advik stared back in disbelief, but Kyra continued. "I know I'll find better friends anyway. Good luck finding friends who will be as tolerant as me!"

Advik scoffed. "Why did you even tolerate me for this long? Just to use me for my coffee?"

"I pitied you, Advik! I could've hung out with my other friends: Niharika, Shriya, Riya! But I stayed with you because you didn't have any friends." Kyra hit back.

"Ha! I never really needed you, you were just way too clingy. Plus, I had friends!" Advik trailed off to name his friends but couldn't recall anyone's name.

"Loner. I don't even care about you leaving anymore. Bye." Kyra stormed out, as Advik watched her leave.

Years passed, but Kyra could never make up for Advik's coffee with another. She made all her friends prepare coffee and tried every coffee shop in small-town Devanahalli. "Café Coffee Day", whose first outlet was set up in Bangalore itself, absolutely anything to rid her taste buds of the taste of Advik's coffee. Kyra eventually ended up convincing herself that she had freed herself from the last memories of Advik. However, a part of her always held regret for what she did. Since she had caused a fight, Advik wouldn't have wanted to keep contact with her, which he didn't. No letters or calls from him. He never came back to Devanahalli again.

In college, while her friends got themselves intoxicated with drugs and alcohol, coffee was Kyra's addiction. Coffee became an integral part of her life when she was feeling overwhelmed, both negatively and positively. Nights before exams were accompanied by mugs of coffee and intense cramming. In exchange for loss of sleep, Kyra graduated at the top of her class from the Accolade College of Liberal Arts.

In the pursuit of jobs, Kyra was offered one in Public Relations in Thane, Mumbai-The city of dreams. Being well aware that it was the same city as the boy's, who never tried contacting her, Kyra didn't want to live there just in case she crossed paths with Advik once again. She accepted the offer from an advertising firm in Kolkata.

It had been a year since she had moved to Kolkata, living in an adequate apartment. The job had long hours and less pay, rendering Kyra to have very little to spend on herself, especially good coffee. However, one rainy morning in June, she was fired for arriving late on the day of an important seminar. Although she tried explaining why she was late, it was raining excessively, and she was unable to find taxis or rickshaws. But her very infuriated boss still fired her.

She walked out of the advertising facility like she had no purpose in life. Then it hit her: coffee. Her best friend. Her companion through her problems, her solution.

"Therapeutic coffee must not be postponed." She thought. Hence, she had a purpose for drinking coffee, she walked to the nearest café: Rito's Coffee House. It was small but a cosy looking place, perfect to stay in for shielding yourself from the ruthless rain.

As soon as she set foot in the shop, she was greeted by the aromas of various coffees. It was so refreshing, Kyra almost forgot that she had been fired moments ago.

"Cappuccino, Latte, Cold Coffee..." nothing on the menu seemed interesting. She needed change—a change in life, in jobs, possibly cities. However, a coffee shop was probably not the best place to look for changes. Kyra proceeded to order a Frappuccino when a Barista told her that she should try the Monday special-"A New Sunshine".

"It's a type of coffee only made once a week, and it has a secret recipe that is unique to our coffee house." The Barista said. Intrigued, Kyra placed an order for A New Sunshine. On receiving the coffee, she first smelt it, out of habit, and it was heavenly, not like other coffees. No wonder it was a secret recipe.

But her nose knew this smell. Too tired to investigate it, she drank her coffee and enjoyed every bit of it. Afterwards, she demanded to meet the Barista that prepared the coffee.

When the Barista came out of the kitchen, Kyra shook his hand and told him that his coffee-making talents were off the charts, unmatched. He thanked her, but before he went back in the kitchen, Kyra stopped him.

"I didn't quite catch your name!" she said.

He turned around. "Advik." He said.

Kyra paused. There was a lump in her throat, and her eyes began welling up with tears. Blinking them away, she said, "Servant?" and let out a broken chuckle.

Advik froze in his tracks. His lips broke back into a smile.

"Kyra?"

"You've changed a heck of a lot since then. I cannot recognise you since the last time you decided to ditch me." Kyra said.

Advik chuckled. "You too, since you misunderstood me."

"I didn't misunderstand anything, I was completely right."

"Were you? If so, you'd know that it was I who incessantly honked the horn of the moving truck to get your attention."

Kyra stared, flummoxed. Advik noticed that she was dumbfounded.

"I never intended to hide anything from you. I was simply grieving and didn't know how to break the news. Plus, you were right. I didn't have friends."

"Advik, you idiot! No, wait. I am the idiot. I'm so, so sorry. I should've understood you better, but I let my ego take over. Although I am not taking all the blame. Why didn't you write to me all this while?"

"Guess you weren't the only one whose ego had taken over." He said.

Kyra ran into Advik's arms.

"Aren't you supposed to be in Mumbai?" Kyra asked.

"I came here for higher studies."

"I rejected a job offer in Mumbai just to avoid you."

"Okay, wow." Advik laughed.

"It took me so much coffee to get over you," Kyra said.

"Coffee helped me feel less guilty about not giving you my address. So, I decided to work a part-time job here as a token of gratitude to it."

"I'm going to need your coffee every day, like old times," Kyra said.

"Anything for an old friend who stuck with me."

"Aww."

"I meant coffee, not you."

"Sure, weirdo."

6

THIS IS NOT A LOVE STORY

by Jaya Prakash A

To attain something in life, it's not enough to just be the person who wants it; we need to be the person who gets it. I was someone who had been riddled with flaws and failed desires that he ended up empty and unhappy. I wanted to be the person who was capable of love, but I ended up as someone who can only want it but not get it. That is why this is not a love story.

"Do you like to swear?" I asked Vidya. It was only a few days after we started talking, but things were looking good. We had enough similarities and shared interests to be comfortable initially, but the varied spectrum of our senses kept us interested in each other. In short, I couldn't get over how cute she was. I couldn't remember how we started discussing profanity on that particular day, but I clearly remember what she answered.

"Yeah, and I can do it in four languages," she chuckled, and I joined in. We were laughing without a sense at everything each other said, and there were barely any awkward silences between our conversations. We literally couldn't be silent when we were together. So we talked about everything from swearing, her taste in music, and how she didn't know whether she liked panda bears or not: I made sure she liked it.

I liked to consider myself as a person who gets to know someone with his body rather than his mind. I did not remember easily where she lived, what she did for work, or how tall she was when I thought about her; hell, even her name didn't pop into my head. For me, that wasn't her. For me what she was, was how my heart raced when I thought about talking to her; how my eyes fluttered, my lips smiled, and my hand danced in the air to an unknown tune; for me what she was, was how she made me feel!

Maybe, I was wrong; maybe, I wasn't the artistic hopeless romantic that I considered myself to be in my head; after all, I would soon break up with her.

***

As I was riding through the city on that fateful day, dark clouds gathered above my head to pour the sweet drizzles on my back which made me squirm on my seat. The wet cloth stuck to my back reminded me of the harsh thoughts that had been clinging to my mind for years and making me lose focus on what was in front of me. Consequentially, my mind started reliving the pain of breaking a girl's heart; the very first time I had to do that to my first ever girlfriend.

As I thought back to my time with her, I did not remember her face but only the ways she had made me feel: how the sound of her name, Riya, matched by heart's beat every time I had heard it; every time something, good, bad, or insanely trivial would happen to me, I had wanted her to be the first person to hear it; every time she would smile, it had made me think how I was the luckiest person in the world, and every time she would cry, I had felt like shit. I had known with utmost assurance that whatever happened to her, she would have shared it with me because she had known that I wouldn't have judged her.

She was the first person to tell me that she loved me more than anyone, and I had told her, so easily, the same thing. I hadn't known I was capable of loving anyone that much until I had met her because it was, she that created the version of me who could love her the way she deserved.

The two years I had spent with her had its ups and downs; we hadn't always been happy, but during each one of those moments, we had never felt alone or unloved. That had been the cornerstone of our relationship. We had been a necessity for each other like air, and that I had found to be beautiful. But that one beautiful thing, the same thing which had made us comfortable and happy, would become the cause of our destruction. It had unravelled us, made us toxic, stagnant, bitter, and unfaithful.

***

As I stopped the bike before a red light, I started thinking I needed to stop living in the past, reminiscing about my wounds, pain, and mistakes. I needed to discover myself or create myself, and become better on my own; become whole.

I finally reached the place where Vidya and I had agreed to meet. Like when space and time are stretched out indefinitely by the gravity of the singularity on the cosmos, the short ride from my home to the café felt an eternity, but I didn't have the mercy of continuing my ride forever eliminating the possibility of hurting her.

I entered the shop, and as soon as my bare moist skin enveloped by the wet shirt made contact with the molecules of cold air inside, she turned her head to look at me. Not in the general direction of the door to see if I had arrived, but her deep black eyes peered right into mine, and it felt like she was saying, "I know you are here," and she wanted me to know that. I was there, and so was she; Vidya, the woman who could swear in four languages and thought she could fix me.

I walked up to her, and even before I sat down, she asked, "Tea?"

I chuckled unapologetically and replied with a smile, "Coffee."

***

We were talking. Each time she said something, I smiled, and when I said something in return, she smiled. The dance of our smiles dazed my mind, but I could feel the time was trickling down, faster than the rain outside, and soon there would be tears; tears heavy with pieces of heart scrapped off from her chest by my coarse fangs would roll down from her eyes, and I already started hating myself.

"You don't think we can do this forever?" she asked while clutching her coffee cup from under with both of her hands as if it's her heart that she is offering to me; to take a sip and realise that it is sweeter than anything I could have ever dreamed about. I believed that.

"I know we can't." I lowered my head and took a sip from my cup. The bitterness filled my mouth, which I wanted to keep away from her life.

"How can you possibly say that without a doubt?"

"I...I can't explain. It all sounds so correct in my head, but I know it won't make sense when it comes out."

"Maybe because it is wrong, have you thought about that?"

"No, it's not like that. It's...the shape of cracks wouldn't make sense to anyone except me."

"What cracks? What are you talking about?"

"You see, you already cannot understand me; it's impossible."

As the words left my mouth, I saw her hanging the head down in retirement, and in her eyes, I saw my defeat, giving up on trying and telling her about the real me. My heart throbbed from within.

"Do you know why I broke up with my first girlfriend?"

She nodded, "no."

"Riya was a smart, beautiful and kind person; perfect in every way possible, but perfect things don't go well with broken things. I said cracks earlier because, in my mind, I see myself as this coffee cup but a broken one. I always have been empty and hurt, so it made sense that I am someone who is broken and can't retain the emotions that he faces in life.

"But she was this shiny, colourful, and smooth porcelain piece that matched perfectly with my broken cup. She fused with me to make me whole, so I could finally keep the few drops of happiness that I was gathering with her. I thought everything was right in the world, and we were happy as we can be, but it wasn't permanent.

"As perfectly logical as it may sound in my head, I know that people aren't coffee cups. They are not rigid; people grow, and they change. And we need space for that. I thought I was complete; whole with her filling my wounds, but I wasn't. That was not life. It's not finding people who make you feel better about your flaws or finding people to be used as your fixing kit. Life needs to be something different; something better.

"If we hadn't broken up by the time when we did, we both would have been broken. So, we let go of each other and decided to go on a journey to find ways to grow, learn, and mend ourselves. To find parts of ourselves, not of others, but our own pieces of our heart shattered across the world to make sense of who we are; doing that and becoming whole is what I want to do.

"But I am broken even after all these years; maybe a little bit better, but still broken and as long there is one tiny crack left in the cup, it will always run out one day." I realised my coffee had turned cold.

"Do you still love her?" she asked, and I could see a hint of tears encasing her pupils.

"That's the funny thing. As fondly as I talk about her now, I don't feel anything for her. The way I feel right now about her is the way I would feel about any stranger that I haven't even met in my life. Once she was gone, you see, all those porcelain pieces which I used to mend myself are gone, and now..." I sighed into my cup.

"You feel broken again," she finished, and I knew then that she understood what I meant by cracks.

"I don't want another repair kit; I want to heal."

"But are you sure that this is the right way? What if you are wrong? What if you need me," she bit her tongue too late to stop herself from talking, and her tears weren't trapped anymore, "what if you need someone?"

"I need you, but you don't need me. As broken and crazy I might be, I do deserve love, but you don't deserve someone who might wake up one day and feel that he has lost his love for you, and I would gladly trade every possibility of my happiness to only one chance of you never getting hurt, and I definitely don't want me to be the person who hurts you. I am sorry, Vidya; I love you too much, even if it's just for this one second, to let me hurt you."

I stood up and walked towards the counter to pay the bill, and she did not follow me; she knew that I wouldn't come back, but she remained seated. I took that as a sign of her acceptance of my leaving, so from where I was standing, on the edge of the atmosphere where she can feel my presence through the air molecules spread between us, I looked at her: one drop of tear escaped my will.

"Will you come find me if you feel that you are whole one day?" she asked while tears rolled down her cheeks.

I didn't have the confidence to nod, so I smiled at her and left the coffee shop. The bittersweet taste of coffee spread from my tongue to heart, and I felt like I might never be able to feel this way again, but fortunately, she wouldn't have to too. Her love was safe from my cracks.

7

THE COLD BREW

by Shaymi Shah

Saira, Sagan, Fayez and Urav had been friends since college. Right from the early morning phone calls to wake each other up, to the mid-day breaks between classes talking over their favourite coffee in the canteen of the college, to the endless late nights of working at Urav's place and being each other's support system in times of need. There were some others too in their group, but they had left the city in search of jobs after graduation- they were all still in touch. Every once in a while, whenever Kiara or Parshva visited the city, they would all catch up with each other.

They were all so different from each other, but it's also what kept their bond alive. Saira was an enthusiastic explorer, someone who always had several different perceptions towards any situation. Urav was someone who thrived on new experiences and was in a constant search for something new that life had to offer. Sagan was generally the quiet observer who would listen more and talk less. He would be engrossed in his work and making sure it was finished in time to be able to get his goodnight's sleep. Fayez was someone who was full of different ideas and could easily get lost in his thoughts. He was someone who could remain aloof for days, but when he did meet, he would always make up for the lost time.

Eventually, Saira got married to Urav while Sagan and Fayez became faculties in the college that they had all graduated from. Saira and Urav would go around the city, explore new places and cafes with them or just go on long music drives in the small lanes of the areas near their college. There were several times when Saira, Urav and Fayez would discuss philosophies and theories related to life in general, sometimes even debate their points of view. They had shared many such moments with each other it was hard to keep track. But somehow, after every such discussion, they had all felt more connected to each other than before. They had often thought how they had managed to tolerate each other all this time and how far they had come together. They had grown and matured with each other's constant support.

Today was one such day. After months and several cancellations of the plans, they all finally managed to meet up. Their college canteen was closed for the day, so they decided to meet at "the new cafe" in the city. While Sagan and Fayez were visiting it for the first time, Saira and Urav had already decided what they were going to order for themselves. They all ordered a blueberry cheesecake and a mango cheesecake, while Saira, "the explorer" as they called her, wanted to taste a different coffee- the cold brew. She knew she might not like it, but she never wanted to miss out on trying something new. They all checked out the place while waiting for the order and soon got to talking.

Sagan: What a place this is! I can't believe something so simple can look so elegant and appealing to the eyes.

Fayez: The beauty is in the eyes of the observer, my friend.

Sagan (rolls his eyes and starts checking his phone)

Saira: I knew you would be dumbstruck by the place. It has been designed by an architect who is just a few years older than us. I hope someday even we end up designing such soulful spaces.

Urav: We've been here, what, like three times this month already and still can't seem to get enough of it. Especially with our friends in design, everyone seems to fall in love with it right away.

Saira: I know, right? I totally agree. I just love the colour palette they have used, it's so coffee-like- brown and black. It completely gets along with the vibe of this space.

Urav: You know what I feel? I think the way they have kept certain parts of the space so raw and incomplete is something very new we've seen. It takes courage to keep the materials in their most raw and pure form without many modifications by humans. I think that's why it's so appealing.

Upon receiving a call, Sagan moves a little away from the table. While Saira being her usual self takes his picture to tease him later.

Fayez: I agree. It's not only about how connected we are to the inside while sitting outside but also how connected we feel to nature here. I mean, look at how beautifully they have framed the sky? It's like it demands to be seen.

Saira: I know! Did you see that small water body they have made on the other end of the space? It completely changes the vibe of this space. It's like there's this smaller enclosed space where they make and serve the orders to keep the cooling inside, but the smaller adjacent spaces are even more eye-catching as their huge volumes are so well contained.

Urav (smiling at what Saira said): How do you make such observations in such a short time? I just love the way your crazy little brain works.

Fayez: Eh! C'mon you two. I like this conversation, don't ruin it. (Both smile embarrassingly). I was thinking about the statement you said earlier, about it being so raw without modifications by humans. I mean it makes me think about us as humans on a larger level. Why should we be called Man-KIND? Don't you think it's quite a shame considering we are anything but kind- to each other or the surroundings in general?

Saira: Here comes our philosopher. (Chuckles) No, I am kidding. I couldn't agree more. I wonder what would have happened if humans never existed. Was our existence ever required here, in this world, on this planet? And why? (She gestures Sagan asking him how long it will take, Sagan, nods showing he will be back in a few minutes, it was an important call)

Urav: What do you mean?

Fayez: What she's saying is just imagine a world where all other living beings except for humans exist- such as trees, insects, animals, birds. Wouldn't they live more peacefully and simply coexist without us ruining their lives?

Saira: Yeah! Exactly. If we were never born, we wouldn't have grown into such selfish beings who, in order to survive, without even knowing sometimes, make their survival so miserable. When you think about it, where does anything come from? Water, air, wind, and land- it's all available in nature. It's free of cost. It's the humans who utilise these resources to make money and run businesses.

Urav: So, are you saying we couldn't live without nature, but nature could easily exist without us? I believe we are doing something great by actually utilizing it. We are the ones intelligent enough to use it to its full potential.

Fayez: But did nature ask us to make it useful? What if it was happy to simply exist for the time it had in this world?

Saira: You know what Fayez, you won't believe what happened last night. I randomly thought of something crazy. I was wondering, what if animals, birds, insects, and plants could actually talk to each other, in ways we wouldn't understand and strategise to come together and end humanity once and for all? That would be so scary, right?

Fayez: I can relate to that. I mean, think about all these viruses and infections that cause so many deaths. Or the natural disasters such as tsunamis or cyclones. They are all ultimately related to a huge ecosystem, right? One small glitch in the system, and it has the power to destroy so many lives.

Saira: I hear you. Let me check how long our food is going to take. She gets up and goes to the counter and asks the guy standing there, "How much longer for the cheesecakes and the cold brew?" He replies, "Just a few more minutes, ma'am. Take your seat. I will get your order at the table right away." Saira says, "Okay, thanks!" goes back to her table and sits down. Sagan is back at the table as well. It seems as though he has been updated about the ongoing discussion by Fayez and Urav. She says, "So it's going to take a few more minutes for our order, where were we?"

Fayez: We were just telling Sagan about our debate. He apparently agrees with Urav and believes that it's the ability to think and our intelligence which makes us different from all these other species. At the end of the day it's about the survival of the smartest, isn't it?

Saira: But how can we be sure that all these other living beings around us don't use their intelligence in order to survive the way they do? If we don't bother them or cause any harm, then they would probably just exist without acknowledging any threats from their surroundings. For example, don't you know about the dolphin's superpower called echolocation that helps them sense their surroundings with sound? Or how dogs can hear a much wider range of frequencies than humans.

Fayez: Yes, all living creatures have a unique peculiarity, but this ability to think is something that could be wisely used, but we choose not to.

Saira: How is it that even if we don't take care of our surroundings, nature somehow selflessly manages to protect and provide for us in every way?

Urav: I don't think I still completely agree, but I shall give this a thought. Since what you two are claiming is something quite abstract. If we weren't born, then all these resources would have just been things.

Sagan: That's true. There wouldn't ever be any advancement in technology. There would simply be an endless, eternal cycle of existence and death of these species.

Saira: Who knows, if we wouldn't have been born, maybe all these creatures would have lived happily and coexisted after all?

Fayez: Or, or, or...just managed to upskill their intelligence, and begin challenging each other in the survival of the smartest rather than the fittest!

Saira: Yes. Who knows? All these stories and theories we create in our imagination, sometimes I wonder if there are others like us who think in the same way. There's still a long way to go and see if any of that could be true. Anyway, until then there's coffee and such conversations that we have over it. Cheers to us and for the endless philosophical discussions that come along.

Ah! Finally, it is here. Guys! Wish me luck. I am trying something new.

The three of them start hogging on the cheesecake and wish her luck as she sips her cold brew.

Saira: Oh my god! This is so bitter. I wonder how long it would take me to develop this taste.

Urav: Probably a week or two.

Saira: Yeah, I don't know. I might just stick to the coffee I make by myself.

8

TWO LATTES - BEGINNINGS OF A STORY

by Karan E

It was a new city for him. With the hopes of a fresh start, leaving behind everything, he has ever cared for in his hometown. Settled in a nice little apartment just a 15-minute walk from where he just started working. But one never gets comfortable in a new city without finding their perfect coffee spot. Not the ever-photogenic Starbucks, Dunkin Donuts, CCD which is always filled with millennials editing their Snapchat stories or those middle-aged people who dive into their MacBook's. Of course, he loved those cafe chains too. But his definition of perfect coffee spot is much more simple.

Those little shops where upon entering drowns the never-ending noises of worldly affairs in their coffee brew. Those shops with dozens of succulents sunbathing over the window. Those shops with dark high-rise ceilings, illuminated by accent lighting hanging overhead. Those shops with wooden cupboards populated with a variety of glassware. Those shops with tableware that convinces you for "Maybe, we can stay a little longer". Those shops where you can hear your coffee grind, smell your coffee roasting, and finally taste that cup of awesomeness all while being at your most comfortable.

Well, he was blessed enough to find one close by, all while resembling his stagnated relationship lifestyle. He starts in the morning from A, his apartment, then he reaches B, the coffee shop, then reaches work at C. What more can we say, He was just the kind of person who found peace with simple things in his life.

Two weeks into his new-found sanctum, a cute female barista starts working there. Yes, this story also explores a girl—a simple girl with her beauty facades over her elegance.

The problem is that guy, he's nervous as a cat. Isn't everyone? He thought to himself! There he was filled with caffeine and his impulsive thinking. Sculpting her gracefulness over in his head.

Days, weeks, goes by. All he thinks about during his sojourn over at his perfect spot is

1. The past he left behind,

2. The woe factor of the day,

3. Think over his life, and it's little to no meaninglessness from which he can't figure out WHY?

4. Maybe sometimes obnoxiously staring at that gorgeous female barista. You start watching her, and she notices too.

He orders the same every single day. He sits on the same spot every single day—the spot where the vines twined over the ventilation shaft hanging from those dark high-rise ceilings. The spot where the thick window glass muffles the busy jargon of the huge new city, he moved in.

The day at the shop was not so busy. There were very few people to attend to. She was there doing what she does best. Smiling all the while attending to worrisome people who order their favourite cup of relief for the day.

Well, today she just handed him his long black with two sugars. One of the few simple pleasures of his life is to have "long black coffee with two sugars". Even on the "It was, I had one of those long, bad days that don't seem to be getting better anytime soon." You can't leave work to go home, and there's nothing else to do except to wait until work is over and head to your local coffee shop.

So, he went in, grabbed his perfect drink, long black with two sugars and sat in. A few minutes later, he looked up. She was there looking at me. Let me just repeat that. He saw her looking at him. And he just couldn't bring himself to look away. He couldn't smile or wave; There he was like a frozen yoghurt. Then she smiled at him. And he just couldn't bring himself to look away.

She was just smiling a little, a simple yet elegant smile, a smile with a twist to it, like the smile of a child who is determined not to weep. Yet it ended abruptly, from a smile directed towards me to a smile with grateful greeting towards a customer who ordered.

Her smile whisked away faster than wisps of smoke dissipated after a candle flame had been snuffed out.

He smiled back at her. They exchanged smiles and chuckles too. Then she looked away, indulging back at her work and he looked down at his coffee. His bad mood of the day disappeared just like the wisps of smokes.

Obviously, he wanted to say something else to her. Wave to her, call her pick, utter some lame jokes while ordering, maybe ask her to write her number on the cup, maybe even asking her to go out with him after work. Well, he did them all. Except he did them all in his mind.

But the conversations in the material world always went like this. Him ordering "Hey, a long with...black with..." while she was interjecting at "...with two sugars", both of them chuckling at the same time. She goes "Here's your order" with that ever-elegant smile on her face. He let his opportunity fly out with wings as strong as phoenix's for a few days.

How magical is that he never found out WHEN he started crushing on her. But he always knew the HOW. How he started painting her in his mind. How he started vividly imagining her allure. How he started musing about her in his words.

She was never the most beautiful girl in the whole world. She was never the one where literature praises as a goddess. But She was all about simplicity, making things easy, helping those around her to relax and be happy with what they have. The simplicity he ventured to find in every aspect of his life. She was the simplicity of her messy bun. She was the simplicity of dark hazelnut eyes. She was the simple denim jean and buttoned-up shirt. She was the plain white sneaker muddied with lustre.

She had a kind of understated beauty, perhaps it was because she was so disarmingly unaware of her prettiness. Perhaps that is why her skin glowed. It was her inner beauty that lit his eyes-that simple yet elegant beauty. If the world can see what he saw, it would also be smarter, wiser, and more importantly experience that serenity she emanated like him too.

It was a little late Friday night, where he was waiting for the weekend to blossom. She didn't have her perfect smile. He knew there was something wrong with her.

Her eyes tragically bore wrongdoings, like they have been poured upon her on a single day. Her lips smiled, greeted those customers, but her eyes ceased to be a part of this world.

Her face once was with russet cheeks like crumpled apple stored in cold weather now was drained with a gaunt expressionless stare.

Her face expressed she didn't care about anything or anyone. Yet the state of her hair said her feelings extended to herself. What should have been curled with tangles held together by a messy bun was dulled. Maybe by the ever running, ever tiring city's recklessness.

His facial expression sank faster. Faster than the keys dropped from the Love Lock Bridge over the Pont des Arts flowing majestically in Paris. His face became pale, like the colour of a moonbeam, or an ivory carving. Every thought in his head pushed to do something about her state. Every nerve wrecked him to say something to her. But right now? No, let it seep deep into the night when moonlight can shine through the window. He said to himself.

An hour later, his perfect coffee spot was almost deserted. He went over to the counter where she stood.

WHERE SHE STOOD LIKE A RAW COLD PIECE OF MEAT!

He initiates a conversation. Hey refill, Please. Here's your favourite brew, she says while handing over his cup. He asks her if she remembers him just from seeing him in this coffee shop. She nodded. He said he thinks that she was upset. And just wanted to know if she was okay?

She nodded again even without lifting her head this time.

He turns back, with a sigh, maybe he should go home. Some feeling in his femoral artery makes him double back. He rephrases his question to her. He just wanted to know if his favourite cute female barista is okay or not? She chuckles. He chuckles too. Breaking the ice, maybe he should have asked for a cold brew.

Her chuckles came back with a reply of I'm fine.

"Sure, does look like you're sad", He interjects.

She glances at him to sit down over the countertop table.

"Well, if you don't mind telling me, what's wrong? Maybe we can both go out a little less sad." He told her with the patience of a well-seasoned listener.

"Only if you drink something other than *A long black with two sugars*", she wasn't about to give in. But he glanced a ray of hope through her smile this time.

“Pour me your favourite brew and then we'll start talking," he replied. Cause he wasn't about to give in too.

SHE BRINGS BACK TWO LATTES.

Did they go on talking all night? Was she the best friend he ever asked for? Was he the go-to person for all her silly talks? Did they become best friends? Did they stay that way? Did love seep into their lives?

How would we know? It is their story. All we got is the beginning of a story.

9

COFFEE WITH A STRANGER

by Arati Harikumar

It was a regular day. The weather was slightly chilly, reminding her gently that she needed to carry her jacket with her. It was her usual routine, visiting the garden close-by. The sun had set, and the streetlights were on, just the right time for her to be with her solitary thoughts for company. As she passed by the fruit seller who smiled at her, urged her to try the fresh apples. She remembered another night in another city with a stranger.

She met him when she was at the lowest point in her life. Her life was falling apart or maybe had fallen apart, and she was watching it as if it was a movie being played out exclusively for her. The last thing she expected was to go on a date with a stranger. When he asked her for a cup of coffee casually, she didn't hesitate. It seemed like someone asked her a rudimentary question, like an everyday question; her name or how is she doing, it was that oblivious to her, there was nothing dramatic about it. And she heard herself agreeing.

Anyone who would have known her recent history would have chastised her for her decision, yet she went with the flow. The flow she always went with. That was who she was. But this was a memory which made her smile today.

It was the very first-time Anandita was living in a Co-Hostel. The year was early 2014. The concept of co-hostel was still new and steadfastly catching up. She didn't mention to her parents that her hostel had men too. In all probability, her mother would have fainted learning this piece of information. And she had enough to deal with. A relationship with a woman that had gone sour leading to multiple threats, leaving her scarred and wounded.

This just wasn't the time for her to say anything to anyone. And certainly not her family.

The other hostelers would have described Anandita as 'aloof', 'distant', maybe even 'stiff' or so she thought. She was either on her phone or with a book, if not, then she would be found sleeping; she ensured her conversation with anyone was limited to just a polite nod or a greeting. Even when she walked, her eyes would follow her feet as if she were counting every step of her way. But for people who knew her, they knew her differently. She was chirpy and happy mostly and even when she wasn't talking, her aura was positive, her energy infectious earning her a nickname of 'sunshine' amongst her many friends and few admirers. But that seemed like a long time ago as if she were someone else. She felt this was a new persona that had gotten embedded to her being, and she didn't wish it to stay. Everything had changed, too soon, and in her own way, she was grasping with what happened.

And then she went for a cup of coffee. With a stranger!

It was by March of the same year, 2014 when she was back home, in Agra where her family had settled since the last 30 years. A few months of living by herself had changed her so much she thought – more emotional than physical. But she was quick to notice the physical changes too. Anandita had finally gotten herself to look into the mirror, and she was shocked at what she saw. She was staring at a pale and tanned face, someone with a visible moustache and extra hair sprouting on her chin and eyebrows which were begging to be threaded. Her hands were rough, and her fingernails were anything but pretty. Her lips were not bruised anymore, but they were so parched that she was afraid of touching them would hurt her. But what shocked her the most was the lack of life in her own eyes, she seemed diminished even to herself. She looked at her pale blue top and remembered she was wearing a similar top with dark blue jeans underneath her black sweatshirt the day she went for a cup of coffee.

Looking back, it was a hideous outfit. It dawned to her that she had not given herself one good look in the mirror for more than two months then. She was only surviving one day at a time. She wondered as she self- examined herself, did she really go on a coffee-date looking like this.

She stumbled on a rock and decided to sit for a while on the nearby bench. Her memories were begging for her undivided attention now. And this quiet time will soon lapse. She decided that it's time for her heart's musings to go on. Picking a dry leaf, she smiled at the memory of her coffee-date.

It was a typical day at the hostel. She was, as usual, keeping to herself, figuring out how she can sort out the mess her life was in. Anandita's ex-live-in girlfriend was making her life hell with repeated calls, messages and even blackmail. Only very few of her friends knew of her predicament, certainly not her family. She had not the slightest idea how she would explain to her family that she was bisexual. Relax, she told herself, it was just a matter of a few more days. Then she would heave a sigh of relief. She would be home, safe and away from this city, with a new job and a new life.

While making her morning coffee, the stranger wished her good morning, she responded quickly before sprinting to her room, she shared with 4 other women. Co-Hostels have a concept of people living together, there are separate rooms for men and women. Thanking God for that, she settled with her coffee on her bed. Her conservative upbringing would never allow her to live in a gender-neutral hostel, she was dreading the day she would have to come out to her family and face the music. As ironic as it may sound, at least she was not keeping the whole truth from her parents.

She met the stranger daily, always in the kitchen and always when she was making something for herself to eat. He would always greet her with a polite nod or a good morning, she would reply hastily and scurry off ensuring there was no room for any further conversation. On that particular day, it was different, or maybe she was different. She couldn't remember what it was, but she was in a better mood. This time she had made friends with the hostel-help who would give her poha on certain days; he was the hostel cook from Nepal. While she was talking to him in the hope of getting lunch too, they met again. What started as a polite nod soon turned to an easy conversation, and before she knew it, she had accepted his offer for a cup of coffee. Kicking herself for being reckless and knowing very well how her family and friends would react, she fervently prayed that he forgets the coffee date. It was just a few hours away, and he didn't. Neither did she. That's how Anandita went for a cup of coffee with a stranger.

What she thought to be a short grab-a-coffee and head back to her solitary bed confinement, turned out to be an affair which included a walk, a cup of juice and another long walk followed by – yes, THE coffee. It could have gone further to more conversations, but then she refrained. The timing was just not right. Anandita was uncomfortable with strangers; she would try to not show it, but it takes her time to ease into her comfort zone.

And here again, it was no different. As she walked and talked with this stranger in a new city, she was at times overcome with fear. She had too many secrets, too much at stake. What if he turns out to be a rapist or a murderer. But as the evening passed and he spoke of his childhood, his aversion for social media and what he does for a living; she sensed herself ease out. For the first time in many weeks, she felt at ease in the company of a friend. She was surprised at the realisation that she thought of him as a friend, and then she mentally kicked herself once again. Just when she thought that the juice had passed off for coffee, he insisted on it - there was a coffee shop nearby, and it seemed only fair to him that he keeps his word. She ignored the tingling sensation which ran through her body when he very protectively put his arms on her shoulders to avoid a car which came right at her while crossing the road. She should learn to crossroads on her own; she chided herself.

Anandita was always a good listener, orator, and a good communicator. One of the early signs if she were comfortable with someone was how her eyes would sparkle as she spoke. She didn't know it then, but that night her eyes did sparkle. The stranger, however, did notice. They spoke at length, and she realised how different their worlds are. He – an aspiring politician, running his business with his brother, evidently from a very influential family and She – well, was none of those and was running away from the city. She could not have told him that. That would be too much for anyone to know. Leaving that part of her life, which she fiercely guarded, she was surprised that she enjoyed the evening. Conversation was smooth, and there was so much to talk – cities they have lived in, the people, the food, the cultures, their journeys to how they met. She knew he noticed something about her, although she could not tell what it was. After a long time, she didn't feel helpless in a company of a completely new person. He seemed genuine, and she felt her shoulders relax and enjoyed her cup of Hot Chocolate, the one he suggested, and she loved it.

The Hot Chocolate was surprisingly perfect. It was neither too bitter nor too sweet. It was rich in texture, creamy but not much, it was just seamlessly amazing for her senses. She smiled in gratitude as he talked on about his family. She noticed how he smiled when he spoke about his mother, of his college and his friends. They spent a good few hours together, chatting about nothing and everything.

Everyone has secrets. Everyone has a story they don't want to share. Anandita was living through one such story. She was scared and nervous; she didn't know where her life was headed, she knew she was being judged and what was worse – she had no explanation for anything, even to herself. She felt like wherever she looked, she was greeted with a mass of darkness. She was engulfed in fear on most days, and she went about braving the storm in any manner she knew. The last thing she wanted was any company, but that night, she let herself be. She learned such a harmless night might never come back, probably never again. She also knew that this was an escape – a very short escape before her fears confronted her before she set herself to find answers to questions that were bothering her, keeping her awake at night.

The stranger she met that night was her evasion- an evasion from the harsh reality for a brief time. He may never know this, but those few hours she spent with him was probably the best few hours of her life in a very long time. For those few hours, her troubles faded, and she could smile genuinely. They never kept in touch. She tried to find him on social media many months later, but as promised by him, he was nowhere to be found. They never exchanged numbers. They never met again. It was like he never existed. It seemed like they never met, never took the long walk in a city unfamiliar to both of them and never had the coffee sitting across each other, talking about their lives. It was also why she never mentioned him to anyone. Only the hot chocolate remained in her foams of her memory.

Anandita's phone rang at the very instant, jolting her back to reality. It was dark now, time to head home. It is amazing how one stranger can lift someone's spirit, she mused as she passed by her regular coffee shop.

Impulsively, she went right back inside and ordered a cup of Hot Chocolate. As she took a sip, she softly mentioned his name under her breath. Thank you, she thought for the introduction to this lovely cup of coffee. It has been her pill of surviving many days and nights. That one evening with the stranger had kept her in good stead for a long, long time.

A lady in the adjacent table smiled at her, and she smiled back. She was reading a book, Anandita noticed that it was the one by her favourite author. The lady looked like she was new to the place.

Coffees have this strange power over us that maybe we don't realise just as yet, she thought to herself as the lady began a polite conversation asking her the best coffee the café serves. Without any hesitation, she suggested, "You must try the Vietnamese Coffee, it's the best here!".

"Sure thing! And why aren't you having it then?", she asked Anandita. Anandita laughed, and the two ladies began a friendly chat.

Another coffee! Another city! Another tale! And life moves on.

10

WITH THAT SMILE

by Anshika Prem Chhatani

Waiting on a bus stand, listening to music, as usual, something unusual happened that day.

"Excuse me? Hii can you please help me out a little", said an innocent voice from behind. I couldn't help but turn around to look back.

White Salwar Kurta and a colourful dupatta. Loose hairs, long, wavy, brown coloured. Her front strand perfectly falling on her face just beneath her eyes. I noticed her, eyes filled with dark black kohl, standing out as if wanting to convey so many stories, waiting for someone to hear them out. She had the most beautiful smile anyone could ever have. She had a little hint of pink lip colour on her lips and a small black mole just to the left side of her nose, colourful long jhumkas and a silver nose pin that can steal anyone's heart. She was the kind of girl that could illuminate any room by just walking in with that smile of hers.

"Yes? How may I help you?" I said after coming back to my senses.

"Uh, actually, I'm new here in this city, and it's my first day here. I actually have an interview with a company. Can you please guide me as to where is this café?" "Café Estaa, Juhu." The address read.

"Um, yeah! Sure, sure! I'm heading the same way, why don't you join me?"

"Really? That'd be great! Thank you so much!"

We booked an Uber headed towards the café.

I couldn't help but lie to her. I knew I did the wrong thing. I wasn't heading to the café but to my own office, but I also couldn't let her go like this. It was after so long, I found a face like her. How could I possibly not know her when she was everything I had ever asked for.

"Café Estaa - where strangers become family!" is what the blackboard out of the café read.

We entered and went straight to the desk to place our orders. She was staring at the menu and I at her. She was just so innocent and beautiful. I couldn't take my eyes off her! The way she was clueless, looking at the menu as if everything written on the menu was of some language that she didn't know to speak.

I could see that hesitation in her eyes when she was about to place her order.

"Hey, do you need some help?"

"Um, yeah, so the thing is, I don't drink coffee. I was always a tea person. So I have no clue what to order? Everything seems so new here."

'What? You've never drank coffee in your life? Don't worry! You can have what I'll have!"

"2 caffe mocha please!"

"Uh, one with three spoons of sugar, please?" How can someone not fall for such innocence? I thought to myself...

I reached my office, but I just couldn't stop thinking about her. With my eyes closed, it was just her face and that innocent voice that could steal anyone's heart.

"May I come in?" said a feminine voice from behind.

I turned to look back and there she was with the same innocence but this time making me fall for her even more. I come back to my senses, and I finally speak, "yes? Come in?"

I could see her surprised expressions. I knew she was shocked. Of course, she had to be, she didn't expect me to see her as her boss. With so much confusion in her eyes, she placed her resume in front of me, I opened it, and the name read Ms. Seerat Kaur.

"So, Ms. Seerat Kaur, Congratulations on finally making it. Welcome to the family!"

"Thank you so much!" she says and leaves.

And just as she's about to leave, 'Seerat? You can call me NK. After all, you're family now.'

With amused eyes, she left to her table, and that's when she received another surprise as if seeing me as her boss wasn't enough, I laughed.

There was a bouquet of fresh orchids and a note that read, "Sometimes, all it takes is a yes and your whole life changes forever! New city, new friends, new challenges. Welcome to the team!" There was also a cup of caffe mocha and another note that read, "It might not be tonight...tomorrow or the next day, but things will get okay. You'll be okay! And until then, you have coffee!"

Seerat just couldn't stop smiling. She was over the top on this sweet gesture. You can see it in her eyes.

After almost a week or so Seerat couldn't help but fall for NK. NK's small gestures towards the company and its employees stole Seerat's heart every time.

Witch each passing day, Seerat could feel herself falling for NK. She wanted to tell NK about what she felt. But her fears stopped her from doing so after all, it was her boss, that she was falling for.

"Congratulations! For you've been promoted to our head office in London" the email read.

I couldn't control my excitement. This was everything that I ever wanted. What more could I ask for. I was literally on cloud nine. Soon my excitement faded. I could see my happiness leaving my body. That big wide smile wearing off my face. Because the mail read that if I had to accept the offer, I had to go by tomorrow morning's first flight. I couldn't stop thinking about Seerat. What about her? I can't tell her about this promotion. After all, I was the only close friend she had all this while. How can I now tell her that I'll be going to London forever?

I decided I won't tell Seerat about the transfer. At least not on her face. I just couldn't. I didn't have enough guts.

Just like any other day, I went to café Estaa around 10. But this time around, I left a note for Seerat. I knew she would be there by 10:10. "I'm not too good with goodbyes. There's so much that I wanted to tell you, but I think there are few things that are better left unsaid. So it ends here. We'll separate our ways and just hope to meet somewhere, sometime in future. And until then, we'll have coffee! Love, NK" The note read. I instructed the staff at the café to hand over this to Seerat.

The same day, Seerat came, she ordered her regular coffee, and just as she was about to leave, the staff called her and handed her the note! She read the note and broke into tears. She was shattered by what she read. In the next moment, without wasting any time, she headed straight to the airport in the hope that she could at least open her heart out. She could at least confess what she felt.

While I was waiting at the airport, an announcement happened. My flight was delayed for an hour. I decided to have a coffee in the nearby café. My mind is still thinking about Seerat. Her face, her voice, the first time when I saw her, everything came flashing back in front of my eyes. I entered the café, looking at the menu, I could only think about her. The way she couldn't figure out what to order and the way she was so precise about the amount of sugar in her coffee.

Keeping all of this aside, I went to place my order, "one caffe mocha please?!"

"One caffe mocha with three spoons of sugar please?"

I turned back, and there she was wearing the same white Salwar Kurta with colourful dupatta and those same Jhumkas with a smile that can make anyone fall for her instantly.

"Seerat? How did you come here?"

"How could I not, Niharika? After all, you left that note for me only so that I could find you."

'So, Ms. Niharika Kapoor, will you be my happily ever after?'

'I'll be your coffeely ever after!'

11

THE COFFEE DATE

by Krupa Prakruthi B

"Hey Jude", was playing when I first walked into this place. I was 17 and was so lost in this little town. I was missing the busy city life and was feeling super alone here. This coffee shop was the only colourful thing in the whole town. It was so fancy and way ahead of its time. I was instantly attracted to it. They had this huge wall of beautiful coffee mugs we could choose from. Mine was always the purple one with little sunflowers on them. They also had fortune beans, like fortune cookies, coffee bean-like stuff with cute short messages in them.

I looked out of the window and saw a bakery where a tea shop used to be. I looked around, so much as changed over the years. These walls used to be purple, but now they are pink, and the playlist is awful. Also, guess what? They discontinued the fortune beans! The only thing that is the same is the taste of this coffee. I took a sip from my mug and closed my eyes. Every time I close my eyes to escape to my happy place, I could almost taste this coffee.

You know, that feeling when you realise that you are in your happy place after so long and it is not as happy as it should be without a certain someone in it?

Well, I'm here today waiting for that someone.

I met him exactly a week after I found this place. It was a regular Tuesday evening; I was drinking coffee and reading Jane Eyre.

"Hey partner in crime!" someone said, and I looked at him with a blank face. He sat down casually at the chair opposite mine.

He then showed me his fortune bean message that said "Go! Meet your partner in crime at Table 5."

"Wow, that's so creative!"

"I know, right!" He agreed "What does yours say?"

I opened mine carefully and it read "The world is a beautiful place if you see it through someone's colourful eyes!"

Like a rare thing, that prophecy came true. We met every day for coffee and instantly became best friends! He used to tell me such colourful stories, most of them probably over-exaggerated truths or beautiful lies. Nevertheless, I enjoyed them. The evening cup of coffee was my day's highlight. None of my other coffee beans ever came true again. Expect for that one time that said, "Always prepare your heart to be broken, nothing in this world truly ever belongs to you." And the barista accidentally broke my constant coffee mug, I was never able to truly commit to any one mug after that.

We at least spend two hours together every day and never really met outside this café. All he talked was about escaping this crappy town and becoming a multi-millionaire. He had an eye for luxury and always chooses the fanciest cup from the wall. Or whatever he thought was expensive.

And one day he just left, without even a goodbye. I waited for so many days in the café for him, and he never turned up. But then I started getting letters from him to the café addressed to me. He wrote to me every week with anecdotes of his crazy little adventures. I was so happy for him but also envied him a lot. Soon those letters turned into monthly and then rarely. The last letter I received said that he was going off the grid for a while and mentioned a mail id for me to contact him in case of emergency.

That's when I eventually stopped coming here. It's been fourteen years now. I never mailed him. But now, I absolutely had to. I wish I hadn't, but there is no way back now.

I want this story to end here. I really don't want to meet him. He is like this known stranger now. How would I even react to meeting him? Say Hi? Hug? Cry? Shake hands? I have no clue. Part of me wishes that he doesn't turn up today.

I was cut from my chain of thoughts by someone running towards me, shouting "Anj!" Wow, this guy is like Paul Rudd hasn't aged a day since I last saw him.

With a moment's delay, I too started shouting with excitement. Well, he hasn't become a stranger after all.

"Are you a vampire? You haven't aged one bit! I thought you would look like an uncle by now." I said as he pulled the chair to sit down.

"Well, I can't say the same about you, Aunty!" He teased.

I made an angry face at him. He laughed. Oh my god, how I have missed this wonderful sound.

"Hey, I'm kidding, don't get mad! He said, Here I got something for you" and pulled out a beautifully wrapped gift box from his bag.

"You didn't have to!"

"But I did!" He winked.

I pushed it aside and told him to get himself a coffee.

He went ahead and chose the simplest looking cup there was and filled it with his favourite kind of coffee.

"Well, this is new!" I giggled, pointing at his cup when he returned to the table.

He looked down and took a moment to understand what I meant.

He smiled. Some strange light entered his eyes.

This reminds me of one of my most interesting adventure stories.

"Do tell!" I said, thinking to myself that it would be some story about how he climbed Mount Everest and took a selfie with a famous rock or something.

But it wasn't.

"Few months back I went on a solo trip to Kodaikanal on my bike. And I stopped at a beautiful yet strange and deserted place." He started.

"Why?" I interrupted.

"To take selfies of course, "he said suppressing laughter. "Listen!" he said with a serious face.

"So there I saw this old man dressed all good, seemed rich but was drinking coffee from this old and almost broken cup. I couldn't help but stare. He caught me looking at him."

"Judging me by my cup, are you?" he asked

"Haha no," I said, feeling ashamed.

"He smiled and asked me to come near him and offered me some coffee from his flask in a paper cup. The best coffee I have ever tasted."

"Better than here, Anj!" He came closer and whispered.

"Haha funny," I said in a sarcastic tone.

"The old man then told me that our life is like these coffee cups. We constantly go looking for the best ones to compare ours with others. But what we forget is that the cup adds no value or quality to the coffee inside. In most times or not, it is just something that hides what really is inside the cup. We should all go looking for better coffee and forget how our cups look for a while. Don't ever forget to think about what you are pouring inside the cup that is what is ever going to matter and slowly walked away from me".

"Wow" I gasped.

"It was Simple yet strange piece of wisdom. It never left my mind. It got me thinking about my cup of life. I can't complain about the luxury I have now, all this money most of it that doesn't even belong to me. But what is inside my cup? Guilt, shame and the constant urge to run away".

He put his hand on my arm. "I'm so tired, Anjali."

I was so prefixed at him and was almost about to shed a tear when my phone blinked with a text message.

"Done?" It said it was from my husband who was actually sitting three tables away from us. "

"5 more mins pls" I quickly replied

"Sorry it was an important message," I said him

"It's ok Anj, I'm so glad you asked to meet me".

"I'm so glad you came!" I said which I know was a partial lie

I took his hand from my arm and said: "you know you can start over, right? This might be a crappy town, but it will treat you well".

"I know! I wish I could, but I don't know how".

There was a brief silence, and it was intense.

"You know what Anj? The anticipation of money, luxury and fun was so much better than the real stuff. I always think about the times we used to discuss what we would do if we won a million rupee. How I would buy so many fancy cars and you a thousand books!"

"And also remember our plans for the beauty and beast type library and a huge screen to watch all my favourite movies?" he said with his face full of smiles and happiness.

I noticed my cheeks hurting, I haven't smiled this much in years. This has been the best day in so long, and I wasn't ready for the next part.

Run! Run! Is all I wanted to shout at him, but it was too late.

My husband came right towards us. He proceeded to flash his batch at him.

"CBI, Sanjay Ram, you are under arrest for money laundering and various other fraud cases."

Sanjay didn't move or resist the arrest.

My husband handcuffed Sanjay, then turned to me and said "" Good job honey thank you for helping the case".

I sat there motionless, all I could think was that my only best friend is going to hate me for the rest of his life, regret ever meeting me and is never going to forgive me for this betrayal ever.

But all I saw on his face was a smile that strangely screamed thank you.

I watched him being taken away, unable to react or even say bye or how terribly I'm going to miss him.

With a heavy heart I looked down at the present he got me. What was inside, made my heart beat a little faster. It was a framed piece of my sunflower coffee mug with the wordings;

To my only true friend,

In this insane world

Memories of our simple moments kept me sane,

Forever thinking about

Coffee, you, and me!

-Love partner in crime

12

CRAZY DOCTOR AND HER COFFEE LOVE

by Deepiga R

All is well until then, there's a coffee. Every morning starts with a liquid hug of my whole beans or roasted, pre-ground powdered 'Filter coffee'. Both of them would go well for me throughout my life. It was always like 'Born to win' - the motto of my life until I entered the MED school. My motto became 'Born to serve' as soon as I stepped into rural camps. The past five years were busy reading books, seminars, projects and now treating patients, somehow, I was always engaged with people. If not, people would find me at Cafe coffee day near my hospital.

I stay in a PG hostel, I wake up early morning by 4 AM, as I am in serious preparation for my P.G. entrance exam as well as in my regular duty. Since I don't get much free time and there is no limitation for my duty hours, I can be called anytime through intercom, so I find my own time by sacrificing my sleep to study more. The best part of my study time is my coffee and the morning climate. Most of the Girls will have a list of steps for skincare as their morning routine. Guess what I have, yes, It's coffee! But not on my face, obviously. My morning routine starts with a perfect coffee. Life was so peaceful amidst so much of struggles when I started having my first sip of coffee. The aroma of those French press coffee would take me to some other world.

My routine duty will be like 12 hours of work on weekdays, few days of Outpatient department and a few days of OTs (operation theatre). Every month ends, I would love to book a room in a seashore hotel, where I can have a beautiful sea view when sunrises and enjoy seeing it while standing on the balcony with my coffee. Still, I always end up spoiling my plans and stay back in my hospital casualty somehow, we guys get emergency cases more at month-end holidays. Though that was difficult, we enjoy working with our senior staff, who is a big inspiration for the present and past young budding doctors. It is cheerful for all of us just by looking at him, showing up every day on time and his dedication.

There is one thriller incident, which was like a fantasy come true in my life, it happened as it is shown in some medical series. I wish to share this cinematic experience in this story. One-night duty day it was, suddenly we got 6 patients from road traffic accidents. And we managed to treat their minor injuries after a few minutes, the real tragedy happened. It was a mass Casualty at 8 PM,15patients, few patients with multiple fractures, one with shoulder dislocation, one with hip dislocation, one among them was brought dead. As soon as possible, all my seniors gathered there, my professors too, non-duty staff, possibly all available staff had come. We have put slabs, cast sutured the wounds and learnt all possible things on that day. It was crazy to see my seniors doing reduction of joint dislocations, fixing them, shifting them to emergency OT.

From learning the names of bones to fixing them, from scared at seeing blood to 'I am used to it,' I have learnt and grown-up. OTs are fantastic, that courage to hold Scalpel, scissors don't come so easy, it's worth the hardship. The way my professor does the surgery, so cool and confident, it gives goosebumps to us, when they provide a chance to assist surgery though we don't do much, it's super classy to be in scrub under OT lights than wearing sarees and diamond necklace. I was just full of joys, fun-filled and also more responsible for the patient. That was the moment I felt how meaningful life is, they were all saved, and the happiest part is me as a Doctor got a chance to save them. After the storm, comes the calm. That storm settled after 2 hours, and all of us went back to have a hot coffee almost around 10 PM.

I was so blessed to work with such professors, who taught us a lot. Not just about medicine apart from that, we have learned how to deal with any kind of situations. After the work, they always take us to lovely coffee shops. Let it be anytime, the coffee shop guy will be happy to see us. Luckily, all of us have the same interests in everything and also, most importantly Coffee lovers. Black coffee with brown sugar is favourite for many of us.

Meanwhile, the small viruses entered our nation, an intense period, all the doctors face in their life. Currently, the hectic day begins with a cup of cappuccino from the mini cafe at the Corner of our hospital. All of us will be like 'Get ready Folks' for the duty, We, The Doctor squad walk inside the ward, amidst that rousing reception as well as unruly behaviour, it's our cappuccino that calms our hearts. Without delay, we dispose of the Cups, Wear the Caps, put on the gloves and corona kit fitted, thus suits on! Our breaths off (sarcastically).

It was not an easy thing for a smart girl who used to be in Starbucks often, so sophisticated with 'Make your own latte' to get suffocated in the PPE kit.

Yet, the service is supreme, and beyond fear, so she chose the arduous path!

With all precautions and fogs inside the face shield, we approach the patients, hear them out, examine them carefully, prescribe the medications with the hope of sending him back to the family. Done with the first rounds of 2 tight hours. Have to write the case sheets and follow-ups. This is all about milder cases. At times, we would be less relaxed, indulged in cafe mocha, which we have specially ordered in the same corner cafe, there comes an emergency call for a severe case, the patient would be struggling to breathe or unconscious lying on the bed. We all have to rush there, senior residents, interns for the golden hour treatment. As soon as the patient gets shifted to the ICU, we hand over the charge and get assembled at the cafe. Nothing can beat that cold coffee after a hot, tiring duty.

As the months passed by, When the cases increased, and most emergency cases came in, New protocols were put up and named as COVID DUTY!

We have packed our clothes vacated from the hostel room, leaving my friends who will get duty in the next turn on alternate basis, now I have to be all alone in a single place since they have allotted separate rooms in hospitals. That was a different feeling when my beloved people sent me inside as if I am going to a war. On Day 1, 6 AM, I woke up in my new room, unusually the room is all for me to use without my roommate. I peeped outside the window, my friends those who had finished their night duty, waiting for me just to wave and they cheered me up. Anything can change in my life, but my coffee won't. I made an instant coffee for myself.

Then I got ready wearing the double PPE kit, triple gloves entering into covid ward, almost all the bed was full. With a mild, moderate, severe case in the same room, then we, a group of covid duty doctors, divided among ourselves and each of us took care of our patients. It takes 3 hours to come out of the ward once I enter inside. Every time we come out thoroughly drenched in sweat, we change up to have a coffee, fresh up again and wear the PPE kit. After 3 rounds of each 3 hours 3/4th of duty get over. And we have our food in between. At the last round, we try our best to discharge a few treated patients. We have 1 round at 3 AM, it was because more people died early morning as per the statistics report. So, we took an extra effort to make sure people are okay. Finally, the 4th round got over, completely exhausted.

Around 5 AM, I will come back to the room and take a quick shower. I will prepare my filter coffee, oh my goodness, how it changes my mood totally different. That's it, I got my life back. Relaxed and all my own time So I will call my parents once in the early morning as they start their working day. I really don't know the theory behind how Coffee can do anything to me. It awakens me when I am supposed to be and make me sleep when I need to. I had completed my cup before going to bed and slept for a few hours as we worked in shifts. The next six days, we faced different cases, but we had the same routine. One-week duty and one-week quarantine get a swab, if negative go back to work, the cycle repeats.

After 14 days of work, my sweet-hearted boyfriend was waiting for me so eagerly because that was the first time we were separated for so many days. As I came out of the isolated rooms, he hugged me and picked up my luggage. He wanted to go places with me and have our couple time back. So, he asked me out, 'Of Course, we are going baby, but COFFEE FIRST'.

Everything will be perfectly fine until then, there's coffee.

13

IT'S A LITTLE LIFE

by Selvakumar Petchimuthu

One morning, Raghu woke up and opened all the windows of his room. He made sure that the sunlight shined all over his room. He went for a morning walk to the beautiful garden, which is closer to his place. After finishing his morning routine, he came back to his room, freshened up himself, and started rehearsing his lines in front of his mirror. He took a bath and wore one of his best shirts, looked in the mirror, and told himself, "You are going to kill today's audition man! Bravo!".

That evening, Raghu came to his room sadly. He opened his wardrobe and looked at his favourite black colour coffee mug. He didn't even touch that mug. He looked at his black colour coffee mug for some time, but he took the blue colour mug next to the black one. He filled his coffee on the cup and started drinking. He started thinking about why this audition went wrong.

Raghu is an English Literature graduate, a young, handsome man with an intellectual and artistic touch. His goal is to become an artist. When he was studying in college, he used to participate in every competition and explored his skills. He was good at doing impromptu. Everyone encouraged him to focus on his acting skills. That's when

Raghu decided to become an artist. He has his own YouTube channel where he posts his impromptu videos and skits. But his goal is to act in a movie.

Raghu has an explicitly good taste in everything. There's a saying that "The most creative people have the messiest rooms." They should just look at Raghu's room. His small room is so full of life. His choice of books, the colour of his wall, wall hangings, Posters, Clock, Coasters, the string light, coffee maker, coffee mugs, Vases, every little thing in his room has a story. He values one thing more than his interest in art. That's his coffee time! He won't drink coffee everywhere and with everyone who asks him for a coffee. If Raghu shares his coffee time with someone other than himself, it means they have a special place in Raghu's heart. Because for him, coffee is a drink that keeps his soul warm.

He makes coffee with Cinnamon sticks, organic beans, almond milk, or coconut milk, Ashwagandha powder, Cardamom, etc.... His coffee has a unique taste, and no one can replace that taste. When someone asks, "Why do you make coffee unique with so many different ingredients?" he would reply, "Because my coffee would feel depresso without them." The ambience he set while drinking his coffee would make anyone fall for his coffee. The fragrance and taste would last for a while. He makes different types of coffee with a different set of ingredients. Every coffee he makes reflects his mood. He reserved his black colour coffee mug for his unique and favourite coffee recipe. He promised himself that the day he gets selected in the audition would be the day he drinks coffee in the black mug. He would look into his coffee mug for all sorts of feelings, emotions, loneliness, love, lust, sadness, separation, etc... That's why his wardrobe has a vast collection of coffee mugs. Most of his cups are imported from many countries with great artistic sophistication.

No matter how positive Raghu is, he was worried that he has not yet had the opportunity to star in a movie. Though he has given his best in every audition he attended, he never got selected. This was happening for the past few months. But Raghu didn't give up.

Another morning, he woke up earlier than usual and started getting ready for his audition. This audition is important to him. They have liked Raghu's self-tape and his short films. So, they asked him to attend the audition for their next production. Raghu didn't want to be late for his audition. He made sure that he had everything planned. If this goes well, it will change everything. Raghu looked at his black coffee cup and told, "Get ready for my favourite secret Coffee recipe!" He was very happy and excited until he got a phone call.

He got a call from an unknown number. Raghu was excited and very nervous." What if the production house cancels or wants to postpone this audition? What if they have found someone? No way! They would never do something like that! Maybe they changed their mind and decided to cast me directly without any audition." A million questions were running in his head, and finally, Raghu attended the call.

"Hello!! Hello...I'm Raghu. Can you hear me?".

The other end of the line was silent. Raghu got confused.

He was about to disconnect the call, and then he heard, "Hello! Raghu...It's me."

"You?? Keerthana!! Wait...you called me? Are you really her?" His voice was breathy and brittle.

"Yes, Raghu! It is me. You thought I would never call you?" She asked in a very disappointed tone.

Raghu started crying and replied, "To be honest, I thought the same. I am surprised that you remember me, and you remember my phone number. Tell me, Keerthana, how is life?"

"You mean my life without you?"

"Because that was the life you preferred when you had a choice," Raghu intervened her.

"Well! I don't like that life anymore. I don't even want that anymore. Three years ago, when I asked you to come to Canada with me, you told me you wanted to focus on your acting and become an actor. But now..." Raghu stopped her again, and he replied loudly, "I am still focusing on my acting, and I would become an actor one day. It's been three years since you left me. But still, you don't trust in my skill, do you?"

"Please let me talk! Don't reply to anything until I finish. Please Raghu! I want to tell you everything. Do you remember how we met? If not for your impromptu in our College fest, I would have never known you in the first place. I didn't fall for your handsome hot face. I fell for your talent. That's how we started talking. We both fell in love because of the interests we shared. I thought all these impromptu and stage shows would end after completing college. But when you told me that's your interest and you want to act in movies. I didn't think it was a good idea. I wanted to spend the rest of my life with you. I can't convince my parents if you don't have a proper job. Even though acting is your passion, I didn't expect that you want to make a career out of it. I thought you cared only about your passion, not me. So, I broke up with you and moved to Canada to pursue my higher studies. But I am not happy here. I never was. It took me two years to understand that doing what you like with the person whom you love is the most important thing of all. I waited for your call, email, message every day. You didn't even try to contact me. I thought you have forgotten me. I was looking at my Facebook memories, I saw a picture of us, shouting happily in our Farewell. And I realised I wanted to be that happy girl again. So, I called you right away. I am not happy here, Raghu. I am not able to focus on anything. I am not living a life that I planned. I miss you, and I miss us." Keerthana ended with tears.

"I'm sorry, Keerthana. I didn't call you because I haven't achieved what I wanted. I didn't have a proper job; I don't even have one now. After everything you told me when you broke up with me, I didn't stop you because I understood the position, I put you in. I respected your choice and let you go. That doesn't mean I don't love you. You have no idea how happy I'm now after hearing your cute silvery voice."

"Let me see how my hero's face would be when he sees me in person."

"Are you waiting outside my door?" Raghu was excited.

"Hahahahaha...I wish! I thought of waiting outside your door. But I wanted to talk before boarding my flight to India."

"Wow!! Please come soon! And How long are you planning to stay here? Tell me it's forever."

"It's forever. I am not going anywhere this time. I am not going to stop you from pursuing what you love. Maybe I would stand next to that senorita mirror of yours and practice your lines along with you. I will wear that possessive girlfriend mask if your heroines are prettier than me. I am going to be there with you for you."

"This is really happening now! Pinch me hard when you see me!"

"Raghu..."

"What?? It was a lie, and you're here already??"

"Idiot! No... Sorry for everything! I love you."

"Keerthana! I don't want to say that I love you! Come here and see it for yourself."

"Wait for one more day! I'll be there," Keerthana ended the conversation and disconnected the call.

Keerthana was the last person with whom Raghu shared his coffee with. Keerthana is the only person who knows about his different coffee recipes. Raghu looked at his clock and realised he was late for his audition. He texted the production house and said that he wouldn't be able to attend the audition. He was so excited to meet Keerthana. He went for a quick shopping and started redecorating his house with all his favourite memories with her. He barely slept until he heard the news. He wanted everything to be perfect, and the day came.

Raghu went to the airport to pick up Keerthana, and they reached his apartment.

"Hey! You ready?" (Raghu kissed on her forehead)

"Let me get my bag, wait!"

"We can get them later. Can I blindfold you?"

"Why???!!!"

"It's a surprise."

"What kind of surprise?"

"A small one! Stop talking." Raghu blindfolded her and walked her to the room.

He took the blindfold off her, and she opened her eyes and saw the painting on his wall.

"OMG..." Keerthana's tears came down.

"Why are you crying?"

"This...This is how I first asked you to be my boyfriend that day. I can't believe you actually painted it on the wall." Her tears came down faster.

"I didn't attend the audition yesterday as I was planning for this. When you proposed to me, I just took a picture with my eyes and saved it in my heart. I wanted to show you that picture. So, I did this," Raghu told and hugged her tightly.

That was the best day for both. Even though Raghu missed that audition, he was happier than ever. The next morning, he woke up and saw Keerthana in the kitchen. Raghu guessed from the aroma filled in his room that she made his favourite secret recipe coffee. She poured it into his black mug.

"You still remember that coffee recipe?" Raghu asked her.

"You still didn't share your coffee with anyone after I left?" Keerthana questioned him back.

"I didn't share because my coffee was special, you know!" He smiled

"Oh!! Not because I was special?"

"You are special! But not more than the coffee I make."

"Your coffee can't give you the kiss that I'm going to give you now." She kept the coffee aside and started kissing him for all the three years they stayed apart.

"I love you, Keerthana! Thanks for coming back to me," Raghu kissed her back, and they started drinking his favourite coffee.

"Hey... Why don't you share your coffee with everyone, just like a normal human? Why do you want it to be special? I mean, it's just a coffee, right." Keerthana asked curiously.

"I don't know either! Every coffee I drink holds an emotion, a memory which only I can associate with it. I won't let it go for any reason." Raghu told quietly.

"So, what do you think of this very moment?"

"Is this really happening? Pinch me now." Raghu laughed; she poured a little coffee on his shoulder. "It's hot, right? It is real, you dummy."

"Not hotter than you!" Raghu smirked.

14

THEIR ACTIVE COMPETITION

by S.C. Elliott

The steel monster had impressively brewed coffee for over a half a century. It belonged in a museum except that it dependably made massive batches of coffee all day long. It was hot to the touch, though the stainless exterior looked as cool as the Silver Surfer.

The waitress reached for a towel to wipe the brown sludge that clung to the coffee mug; wiping it around and around in perfect circles. She thought back to the instructions, *two coffees, two Sweet-N Lows.* Folks were more than happy to specify. Coffee was a sacred ritual in these parts.

Almost as an after-thought, she stacked the ceramic mugs next to the plastic caddy full of sweeteners on the tray. She had fixated on one detail and almost forgotten the most important part.

The coffee was the most pleasing aromatic. It had a calming almost psychological effect in the restaurant. The steam tumbled out and beckoned like freshly baked pie in an old cartoon. The couple lit up when they saw their coffee. They used their last bit of energy to summon wide smiles.

Must be their first cup, she thought. The waitress dropped off their mugs and sugar caddy. She walked away to allow the coffee time to sink into their bones.

Jim stared at the couple for a brief moment.

"Did you see that?" he asked.

"See what?" his daughter Mel replied.

"Those two were served before we were."

The woman glanced over her shoulder at the couple who gingerly sipped at their coffees as if drinking a delicacy. She laughed softly. "They were here before us, Dad."

"That doesn't matter. Look at what time it is. I'm dying here. I need my morning, Joe."

"Look." She pointed behind him. "There she is. It just took a little bit longer because I ordered something special."

One by one, the drinks were unloaded onto their table. Mel reached for her icy concoction and took a sip of the refreshing beverage. "Ahhh. Perfect. Thank you."

"Do you need a menu?" The waitress asked.

"No, thank you. We're just here for coffee."

The waitress wandered off with the pot of coffee; stopping by every head positioned pertly above the vinyl benches like cherries on ice cream.

"What is that?"

Mel quirked her eyebrow. "Coffee."

Jim pushed his coffee mug forward. "No. This is coffee. That's fru fru coffee."

"Fine, it's fru fru coffee."

He settled into his chair, pleased with her acquiescence. His hands wrapped around the mug, the heat of the brew warming his old bones. "Maybe we should have gotten a menu."

"Why?"

"We came all this way, might as well get breakfast while we're here."

"Are you hungry?"

He shook his head. "Does that matter? I'm hardly ever hungry anyway."

"You can order something if you want. I'm not hungry, though."

"Everyone else is ordering breakfast."

Mel looked around the diner. Everyone was either eating, ordering, or hungrily waiting. "Order yourself some eggs then."

"I don't want eggs."

"Order whatever you want."

"I don't know what I want." Jim looked over at the couple who had arrived a scant minute before they had. "What do you suppose they ordered?"

"I don't know."

"They look as fru fru as you."

"Dad."

"Mel."

"I didn't hear their order."

The waitress came back and topped off Jim's coffee. She looked expectantly at Mel. "Would you like another ice coffee?"

"No, thank you. One's enough."

"You're a one-cupper, huh?" The waitress asked.

"I suppose so."

"Ma'am," Jim spoke.

"Yes, sir?"

"What did that couple order for breakfast?"

The waitress turned to look at the booth a few tables away. "They ordered the corned beef hash and eggs."

"We'll have two of those."

"Dad!" Mel reached across the table to catch her father's attention. "I'm really not hungry."

"We'll have two of those," Jim said emphatically.

The waitress nodded and walked away. Clearly uninterested in getting in the middle of their spat.

"What were you thinking?" Mel asked.

"It sounded like a nice thing to try."

"It's not a competition."

"I know it's not."

"Then, what is it?"

"I'm just enjoying myself. I don't want us to leave." Jim remarked.

"We could stay here and drink coffee as long as you like. You didn't have to order anything else."

He nodded, though unconvinced. "What do you suppose those people are about?"

"I'm sure they're about many things."

"Make something up about them. You're really good at that." His nose disappeared into his coffee on the next sip.

Mel covertly looked at the couple, who by now must be aware of her father's fascination. "Her name is Zelda. She's a retired artist and shop owner. She sold her artisanal bakeware company to their only daughter Billy."

"Why the name Billy?"

"They only wanted one child. Since Barry couldn't have a boy to pass on his legacy, they settled for a unisex name."

"William is a man's name."

"And Billy is whatever I want it to be. Who is making stuff up? You or me?"

He waved away her complaint. "Fine, fine. Tell me about Barry."

"Barry likes corned beef hash and black coffee."

"No fair!"

Mel looked over at the man's blue cardigan. "Barry is a retired calculus teacher. He taught in the same school all his career. His sister was the principal there, a real ball-buster that one."

Jim's laughter was more of a choking snort. "You see? You're great at this."

The waitress appeared with two piping hot plates. She set them down then nervously disappeared.

"Do you want more coffee?" Mel asked.

"Nah. I'm a two-cupper. You?"

"No. I hope I can force down some of this food. It smells pretty good, actually."

"What were you expecting?"

"I don't know. The word "hash" always conjures up this image of last week's medley we need gone ASAP."

"Maybe sometimes. Not this though. Look at them." He subtly motioned with his brow to the table that had become their active competition.

"What now?"

"Do you see them looking at us? The tables have turned."

"What's that supposed to mean."

"Look at their table."

She did. "Yeah? Am I missing something?"

"Do you see any corned beef hash?"

"I don't."

"We were served first." Jim sat back, triumphantly.

15

CHAI OR COFFEE

by Padmashri Jayaprakash

How good it is to have a cup of chai in this pleasant weather and to look at these tiny droplets of rain. Nothing is better in life than a hot cup of tea, a nice view, and rain," I exclaimed when my mom was making tea for me. I am relieved because the devil in my house is sleeping peacefully. I have a brother, and he loves Coffee, nothing but Coffee. I don't like him or his Coffee. He is sleeping for a very long time now; he must be dreaming about owning a coffee estate or something about Coffee. Weird... I know, right.

I can bear him to some extent, but not his Coffee. Everything in the world revolves around Coffee for him. He demands a cup of Coffee for everything. I can't stand his Coffee freakiness, but I don't know why my mom or dad isn't doing anything to stop this madness. Then I looked at his Coffee mug. It is just an incredible, pitch-black coloured mug with the quote, "Coffee addiction is just normal." "Coffee addiction is normal, but are you?" I shouted as I was tapping his shoulder to wake him up. His love for Coffee scares me. He is fourteen years old, and his notebook is full of stickers like "Coffeeholic, Coffeefreak, Coffeezoned, Pothead, Procaffeinating, Caffeine Junkie" he has written a lot in his book. His handwriting is terrible, so I am not able to read everything. But I know for sure that it would be about his Coffee or the "love" for his Coffee.

He is still asleep, and my mom came with my tea. I was wondering if he grows older, it would be my responsibility to find him a girl who loves Coffee, else he would never get married. Who cares if he'd get married or not? I started drinking my tea while enjoying the rain.

"Baby…where are you?" My father was calling me. I finished my tea already and went to check with my dad. "Yes, Papa…!" "Listen, Shri! Sadhana's birthday is coming up next week. Both of you get dressed and buy a gift on your behalf to your little cousin sister," he told me and gave me the wallet. "But Papa…both of us? Me and Mama, right?" I wanted to verify, and he replied, "No…We have other work to do. You and your Brother have to go now. Wake him up and get this done" My Nightmare started right after he finished the sentence.

Sadhana is a year old now. I can't believe she is one already. I have come across many new babies, but Sadhana is different. She is like the beginning of all things-wonder, hope, a dream of possibilities. The calmness in her face always tells me a story. I can look at her face all day. She is a precious gift to me. Now it's time to get a gift for my little princess and to wake up my little devil. My dad left me with no option; I have to go with him. I hate shopping with him because he talks too much about Coffee and would stop in every cafe to read the taglines and to take pictures. He is a garrulous fellow, the type of loquacious that he could not stop talking about Coffee.

"Hey, Man! Hey Monkey…Hey you!! Enough, get up," I was bawling out at him. He wasn't even responding. "We have to buy a gift for Sadhana's birthday, and Dad wanted us to leave the house right now, does drinking too much Coffee make your ears deaf?" I yelled loudly. Then he wakes up immediately. "Hey, idiot…I will refresh myself and get ready; I want Coffee right now. Hurry up!!" he ordered me as if I was asking him to pick an early birthday gift for me. "You never give up on your Coffee, will you? It's your sixth Coffee for the day. Go…google about what happens if you drink a lot of coffee," I shouted at him and was preparing Black Tea for him. I would love to mess with him more, but right now, Sadhana is my only priority. My definition of heaven would be irritating him. I am Jerry, and he is Tom. Guess what? Jerry always wins.

"Hey...where is my Coffee??" he came eagerly with his incredibly beautiful black mug. He was disappointed when I poured Black Tea into his cup. "Shri...it's Tea, pour it in your up...where is my Coffee," he asked angrily. "No Coffee!!! Papa said you had enough coffee for the day. You can have this Black Tea or Nothing. That's what papa told me. Shall I call papa now if you want to confirm the same?" I told him casually and was laughing inside. He didn't say anything as he is very much aware of the fact that Dad will never encourage his Coffee obsessions. He drank the tea quicker than I expected.

I am happy that I have finally made him skip his seventh Coffee for the day. I started driving the bike, and he was sitting in the back seat. I clearly told him not to disturb me while driving when he sees any coffee shop on our way. He nodded and sat quietly. I was surprised because he wasn't arguing with me. My Black Tea has some magic, I believe. We reached our favourite gift shop, "World famous Love article," in twenty minutes. He was at his best behaviour till the very moment. No Coffee talks! Nothing!

"Storm after Calm!" My Fourteen-year-old brother is going to do his part to make justice for the quote. I was planning to gift her a bracelet, but he was planning to buy the little, tiny coffee mug for her. I lost my temper and told him, "Not everyone in our family is a Coffee freak, and what a one-year-old girl has to do anything with a coffee mug, now? Don't get me started. Please behave yourself and help me get a good gift for her." We parted our ways apart and started looking for the gifts.

I was looking at Rattlers, Musical Toys, Baby Blanket, Socks, and a lot more. Then I saw a Baby walker, and I decided to buy it. I don't want to discuss it with my little devil brother because he would start arguing with me for selecting that small coffee mug for her. I asked him to join me at the counter. Dad texted me, "You two buy whatever you want for yourself. Love, Papa" That's my Dad! I was trying to hide the phone, but my brother saw the message. He was asking the shopkeeper whether they could customize the Cradle I selected. "Wait...what?

Why do you want to customize this?" I stopped him angrily. "Dad asked both of us to choose a gift which we like. You bought Cradle. Did I object? Why are you objecting to me every time?" he started fighting with me. "Do whatever you want. I will be outside" I left the shop and texted mom everything happened.

He customized the Cradle with the sentence "As sweet as Coffee" and bought a bag full of things for himself. I didn't even check the bag he purchased because anyway, it would have something to do with the Coffee. We left the shop and reached home. I was waiting for my mom to shout at him for his behaviour at the shop.

She asked both of us to sit together on the sofa. She said, "Your sister is leaving home in another one week for her college. You will start missing each other soon. That's the reason we asked you both to buy a gift for Sadhana. We thought you will have fun together and help each other in choosing the right gift. But what have you done? When will you two stop fighting over Coffee and Tea? It's evening already. Both of you settle down with one drink, either Coffee or Tea. I can't make two different beverages for two people. I will give you two minutes to choose one, else you would end up drinking nothing".

Without any second thought, I shouted, "Coffee," and he screamed, "Black Tea." My mom was surprised. He opened the bag he bought from the shop for himself and gave a box to me. I opened, and there was a black mug inside with the line, "Will you be my coffee companion?" I was shocked and hugged him in tears. I replied, "I love your gift. But darling, apparently Coffee is not my cup of tea". He started crying and said, "I know!!!! I love you, and I am going to miss you so much". My mom captured that moment on her phone and sent it to Dad. Dad replied, "That's my Children!".

16

SINFUL BLISS

by Archana Natarajan

They say that the period between engagement and marriage is one of the most exciting phases for a bride and groom-to-be. I wasn't feeling any different from the day we celebrated our Platinum Day of Love. After being in a long-distance relationship with Adi during our courtship period, I felt the urge to meet him and get to know him better before I could feel confident about him. Who would have imagined that a couple who got to know each other through a dating platform like, *Aisle* ended up getting engaged through a horoscope match too? We both had decided to bury the *Aisle* secret and go ahead with the regular proceedings as it pleased our parents. Once a relationship clicks, who cares if it is *Aisle or Bharat Matrimonial.*

Our relationship was chugging like a steam engine, thanks to those miles that separated us. True love doesn't get diluted with distance, but we were yet to discover it. I tried my luck at job opportunities in Bangalore where he was staying so that I could get to know him better before we were officially engaged.

Our story from courtship to being engaged and then getting married was a strange one because our lovable moments always had something to do with food. I used to fear at times thinking that our gluttonous trait could affect our health, but we balanced it well just by promising to have an active lifestyle, just as we did with our relationship.

The first day I set foot in this city, I got a surprise welcome by Adi with a bouquet of twelve roses.

'These are for those 12 months which we have known each other for,' he said, squeezing my hand.

It was extremely chivalrous of him to receive me at the railway station at 3:00 AM on a Sunday morning when he would be otherwise happily sleeping. The excitement to meet me had weighed over his love for sleep. I had put on my worst look that morning. He came close to me holding the bouquet, and we embraced each other for the first time. It wasn't an awkward feeling at all. It felt as if we had known each other for a long time.

As we sat in the car and picked up our conversation from where we had left on the phone last night, he decided to take me to a coffee shop knowing that I love coffee. I was wondering if there would be any coffee shops open at this wee hour? We were lucky that a 24x7 Café Coffee Day was open. I had never seen a CCD more beautiful as this; It was a small garden café. We had to wake up the server boy and ask him for piping hot Café Mocha which happened to be our favourite. As we sat at a cozy corner table in the garden sipping our coffee, an aroma of first love wafted into our souls.

How could I forget that morning, as we sat with our hands entwined, sipping the nerve soothing coffee at the crack of dawn looking at the crimson sky and enjoying each other's company! It was certainly a date to remember. Freshly ground coffee beans have magic in them. The aroma is strong enough to mask any form of fragrance that lingers around. That's how our feelings were at that moment. There wasn't even a shade of doubt that we had about each other. Things were seeming perfect the very first day, but coffee concoction when not mixed in the right proportion with milk and sugar can leave a bitter taste in the mouth. So, I told my heart to stop pounding so hard and let my brain take charge. The coffee did wake my brain up from its slumber to register the precious moments of my first date with Adi.

I finished my coffee quickly and looked at Adi sipping the last bit from his mug. He caught me staring and asked, 'You want some more?' Just for the sake of having a sip from his coffee mug, I took the last gulp. The after effect of it was something that I had never imagined. The next moment, warm lips, smelling of coffee had engulfed mine, and before I could open my eyes and realise what had happened, Adi was standing by the car waiting for me to get in. The motto of CCD - ***'Anything can happen over coffee'*** was proven right for me.

Adi dropped me at the paying guest accommodation and left, allowing me some time to settle in. I kept thanking my lucky stars for getting me a job in Bangalore because our relationship was getting a chance to blossom. My thoughts were all over the place the entire day. I could still sense his lips on mine and the smell of coffee that hit my nostrils when he came close to me. It was having an intoxicating effect on me.

Our long-distance relationship continued even though we were in the same city. We waited for the weekend so that we could spend more time with each other. It was exciting to plan for the weekend as soon as the week began. Weekend outings in the city were just a pretext to meet and get to know each other better. We tried to go for movies that interested us, visited book shops where we could read or discuss our favourite books, attended music concerts, went partying, met friends, tried to find out activities that we both liked and all of this was done over a cup of coffee or tea on weekend evenings.

We were the so-called foodies. That was the first among the many other common similarities and likings that we had. Although the cuisines that either one of us liked were not completely the same, but we were able to discover our love through food. Initially, we spoke only about our favourite dishes, likes, and dislikes, but when we were together it was exciting to try out something new. It is said that food has an impact on the brain directly. The gastronomic delight one gets after having their favourite dish has the same effect on the brain as the feeling of being loved by someone.

It was New Year's Eve, and Adi had invited me home to join him and his friends in the celebration. I had never attended a New Year celebration party until that day. I was a little hesitant in going to his place and being with friends, but I agreed only because his friends were also bringing their respective girlfriends' along. The apartment where he was staying with his friends was a beautiful one. It was the first time I was entering a house where only men stayed, and I was feeling awkward, even thinking about it. There was music, good food, and creative homemade cocktails made by one of Adi's friends. I spent more time observing Adi around with friends than talking to anyone much. His friends were too excited to know about our relationship. That's how our conversation continued.

I felt a little relieved seeing that Adi was his usual self when he was with his friends or me. There was no dual personality that he adorned at least in front of his close ones. It was one of those questions which I had in mind before I could take the relationship forward. Not that I had an option to step back! It was only one additional reason to feel happy about the person with whom I was slowly falling in love with. We waited for the clock to strike 12 and welcomed the new year wishing each other good luck and happiness. Adi's friend challenged us, saying that as we all start the countdown to welcome the new year, we should all have a Tequila shot with each count. Since there were 10 seconds left, we were all forced to have 10 shots continuously. I think that was enough for us to not be our normal selves for that night. Adi still seemed a little sane, but I wasn't. I became extremely quiet but went with the flow, not knowing how to react. I was never used to having alcohol, and 10 shots were not something which my body could take. Thankfully, nothing happened to my health, but I swore that day that never in my life would I have so much alcohol.

I have never been so quiet, but it made me calm down so much that even Adi found it strange. The celebrations were almost about to end as none of us could stay awake because of the overdose of alcohol. Amidst the confusing discussion that was happening whether the girls should go to another apartment and stay over for the night, Adi took his chance and stole me from the group and took me to the terrace.

The dark sky was illuminated with brilliant colours emitted by the firecrackers. The chaos caused by the crackers was loud enough to get people out of their beds and celebrate the new year. But, for some reason, I was at peace at that moment on the terrace as I stood close to Adi admiring the lit-up sky. Adi pulled me close and gave me a tight hug. He cupped my chin with his hands and lifted my head so that his lips could meet mine. Our lips smeared with salt that was left-over after the tequila shots met each other. The strong smell of alcohol and the taste of salt against our moist lips made my stomach churn with desire. That day was one of those very firsts when I saw the most romantic side of Adi. A strong and a passionate kiss to ring in the new year with firecrackers in the sky made me feel as if life were a fairytale. I had to push him away just to breathe and absorb myself into that moment. We did not speak, but our eyes gleamed with the reflection of the bright sky.

Realising that it was quite some time that we had spent on the terrace, we both rushed downstairs just to make sure the others did not realise our absence from the scene. I had to go with the other girls to their apartment to stay over for the night. I had no heart to leave Adi and go, but I had to. He had left a desire burning inside me, and I needed to wait till the next day to extinguish the fire.

I wanted to text him and describe to him about my feelings, but I did not have words to do justice to them. My head was reeling with passion, and my palate was burning because of the strong shots of Tequila. It took litres of water to flush out the intoxicating effect of alcohol from my system. But how was I supposed to stay normal after what Adi had done to me? All I could remember about the previous night was the strong salty kiss that lingered in my senses throughout. The long-distance courtship had taught us trust more than love.

***

I was trying to recall a few more instances when the trail of thoughts was disturbed suddenly.

'Do you want some more of this?' Adi asked while feeding me and our little one in the making, a spoon of chocolate brownie with ice-cream.

It was 1:00 AM, and we were at the same CCD, where we had met each other or the first time. We were sharing a sizzling brownie with ice-cream this time, thanks to the midnight cravings. A spoonful of hot chocolate over soft and warm brownies with vanilla ice-cream was enough to make me fall in love with Adi all over again.

17

HOLD MY HAND

by Saranya Dhandapani

It was Monday and the last day of 2001. I had to travel 32 kms everyday up to my college. When I finally came home, I just wanted to eat, cuddle myself, and sleep. In the past three hours, I have been scared by the buses that thunder past me, turning precisely where they should, like a mammoth with a cheetah's precision. The traffic was worse. I didn't want to have any small talks with my parents. I was tired of my long travelling. Sometimes I wish I would have chosen home learning or remote learning. But I wanted to explore this new city and adapt to this culture. There were no hostels or apartments nearby my college. That was the only college where I could go. So, I had no options left. I have never told my parents about my exhausting daily travel. If I tell them, they won't let me go and set me up for Remote sessions, which I absolutely didn't want.

That day I came home, I was tired more than ever. Somehow, I managed to reach home at 11PM. I had everything planned for that night. "Have dinner, no small talks, hit the bed," I kept saying it to myself until I heard his voice. I have had a very sharp and enhanced hearing since birth. I can even size up people just by hearing them. When I listened to the show for the first time, I felt it was a special note which is going to change the rhythm of my whole life.

"Have you heard this song by Vairamuthu? 'Want a brand-new world! Want a new sky every day! Want a shower of golden coins! Want the birds to sing in my favourite language!'. Times might roll, days might go faster, hours would go even faster when we are asleep. But I always believe there is the deepest connection between my voice and your ears. With that hope, I will start my 2002, and I am going to own it. The lyrics I told at the beginning of the show, I thought, where he got the inspiration for this song. Then I remembered my favourite poet, Bharathiyar's lines.

"I need a small piece of land, Oh divine mother, A small piece of land, and there,

In the midst of that small piece of land, you should build me a house with,

Four pretty pillars and several floors and there near the small pond,

Coconut tree leaves should shine in small plants.

Near ten or twelve coconut trees, moonlight should come

Like a shining pearl and there the soft song of the nightingales,

Should come and fall in my ears to make mind happy,

Good light breeze should blow to make me further happy."

How could one desire like this? Even if they could desire, how could one write about them with every little nuance? Only he can write like this. Such effortless, beautiful writings are very rare nowadays. Can anyone's writing journey be complete without getting inspired by him?? We always want more. We would always end up wanting more. But have we ever thanked enough for having everything that we have now? We will continue to talk. Until then, stay tuned. I am your Saha! It's Hello FM! 106.4"

I lost all track of time as I lay on the floor, curled into a ball, and started thinking. I never enjoyed anyone reciting Bharathiyar's poem until I heard those lines in his voice. This isn't the movies, I remember telling myself, but why everything around me was frozen in place and why did time slow down. I could only hear him talking as if I had blinders on. He reminded me of the poems, stories, magical and complex, each feature of his voice hiding a different story. Only if I could capture his voice and draw sketches with it. My mom looked at me and asked, "Hey, Anne! It's late already. I'll bring the dinner here."

"Yeah, mom! How long have you been listening to this show? How come I have never heard this?"

"Every night, your dad and I would listen to his show before going to bed. You liked it?" she asked happily.

"He quoted my favourite poet's lines! Have you noticed the background music, mom? It's Sahana. That's my favourite raga, and it's the rarest. His voice is so mellifluous. His voice, the BGM, and the way he talks. It's so soothing. I totally forgot that I had to eat supper and sleep. I guess I could spare some time tonight and listen to this."

My mom went to the kitchen and brought food. My dad increased the volume on the radio. We three sat together and waited for the song to end so he could start speaking.

Song ended. We adjusted our sitting position and prepared ourselves to listen to his story. It was so different from the other shows on the radio. He didn't start with, "Welcome back!" or talk something about the song that played before. Nothing! He just started talking from where he left.

"But have we ever thanked enough for having everything that we have now? When your mom makes your favourite Pancake or Dosa, you don't have to gift her a gold ring or a bracelet. Just kiss her and thank her. Have you ever thanked your friends for constantly tolerating you and your ranting? You can't thank them! But hug them and tell 'You know what? The biggest problem in my life is YOU, and I absolutely don't want to get rid of that'. That's what best friends are for, right. Kiss and sniff your wife/husband. That's how you could thank the love of your life for being everything to you. This year is going to be great. But let's thank the universe for what we have got now!"

My tiredness was gone. I slept peacefully that night, imagining Saha in a quaint old country house, reciting my favourite poem and telling me stories that I never noticed. I kept playing his voice in my head because I didn't want it to stop. He gave me a new perspective to enjoy my boring little life. I slept happily that day, knowing that I've a lot to celebrate and be thankful for in my life.

Ever since that day, my routine has changed. Sometimes, I thought that just his voice was beautiful enough to spend one lifetime just listening to it. I wondered how lucky his family or the people around him must feel to have someone like him. I never went to bed before listening to his show on the radio. Life was good! The name of the show is "Diary with Saha." In the Tamil language, the word 'Saha' means a fellow friend. He recites every common man's story in a beautiful way where anyone can easily get connected to it. I became a huge fan, and I loved his voice a lot. I have painted a face in my mind for that beautiful voice. That show was very famous in our times. Many of my friends tried to find him and invite him to our college events. But I wasn't involved in any of it. I was very happy listening to his show every night, and for me, he will always be the man I pictured in my heart and mind.

One day, he was talking about Coffee. Coffee is such a fascinating topic, and he started giving so many stories about Coffee. Out of all the stories he told that night, this is my favourite. "Consider you've invited 18 to 20 guests to your housewarming party. Give them Coffee in different kinds of cups!!! (Crystal Cups, Glass Cups, Ceramic Cups, Shining Ones, Some Plain Looking, Some Ordinary & Some Expensive One) Everyone would think that you may not have the same kind of cups, and due to the large number of guests, you've served the Coffee in different cups. When all of them had a cup in hand if you notice all the nice-looking & expensive cups are taken up, leaving behind the ordinary, plain, and cheap ones!!! It would be a surprising moment, as nobody noticed that there were some extra cups of coffee, and while having their cup, nobody took the ordinary cups, and all of them were left on the serving tray". Saha continued, "Every one of us wants the best cup, and that is the source of our stress and tension. What's inside the cup is our little life. You must learn to make your own coffee and pour it into any cup as you wish. But remember, our priority is the Coffee, not the cup."

I neither had Coffee nor made one. I was 23. I have pulled all-nighters, prepared ridiculously for my semesters, and enjoyed pie. All in all, I've spent 23 years living a very normal life. Except, I did so without the company of Coffee. After hearing his coffee talk with my favourite raga in the background, I wanted to try Coffee. I always wanted a reason to try new things in life. I tried many new things in life because of him. I started reading many books, travelled alone, went for a road trip, and I even started sending letters to my special person in their special days. It isn't just the memorable way to touch the people we love but also the effort we take for someone to make them feel special. I used a Picht typewriter to type my letters, and my dad used to deliver those on behalf of me. I smile every time I remember the days I listened to his show. It was the best day of my life. I started enjoying the hidden beauty of this world through his words. Out of many things I tried because of his show, my favourite is Coffee.

The show was stopped after 2010. It's been ten years since I have heard Saha's voice on the radio. I am 40 years old now. The only thing I could hold onto in my life is his voice. Saha always told in his show that this digitalized world would miss so many beauties of life. This generation would never realise the joy of writing handwritten letters and delivering it to our loved ones on our own, even if it takes hours of travelling. He was right. My daughter would never understand how much that radio show meant to me. She always sits in her room, doing something with her iPad and MacBook.

One day, my daughter came out from her room, screaming, "Mom! Is this the radio show that you used to tell me about?? Someone published his shows on YouTube two months ago. Come on! Listen, Listen!!!" I was surprised and shocked. It was indescribable how I felt when I heard his voice again. The voice that has been in my head for almost 17 years. It reminds me of the first time I listened to the show.

It reminds me of home, dad, and mom and the smell of her Coffee. I spent the next six hours listening to Saha, and it felt like I found my lost baby. I asked my daughter to teach me how to listen to this every night like I used to do in my college days. She brought me "Alexa" and taught me how to use it.

Next night, I prepared my coffee, went to my terrace, and listened to his shows all over again. His voice has always been my guiding light. With the help of it, I have never felt sad about the lack of light in my eyes. I stopped worrying about being blind when I was 23. That was when I started listening to the show. I have felt the serenity and purity of this whole world because of him. I don't want to know how this world looks like. I don't want to know how my coffee cup looks like. For me, what matters the most is the Coffee in it and the life I live. The most practical reason and the only reason I like to drink coffee is that it kept me awake when I wanted to listen to his shows at night. Later it became a habit. Listening to his voice and having Coffee. When the show ended, I was left with Coffee and his memories.

The perk of being blind is that I get to enjoy every sip of my Coffee. I never cared about the size of the mugs. I randomly take one cup closer to me and pour Coffee until it gets filled. And I drink the Coffee until the cup gets emptied. As Saha says, you got to enjoy every moment of your life. You will never know when it gets over!! I neither know when my cup gets empty nor when my life ends. I don't know what I see when I hear his voice. But it smells Paradisiacal.

Thank you, Saha, for giving me everything! Thank you for adding colours to my boring little life! Thank you for introducing coffee! Your voice will always be my favourite! You're the song stuck in my head, and I'll always listen to it with my favourite coffee. Thank you for holding my hands and bringing up the light which chased away all the darkness in my life!

18

LIFE WITHOUT FILTERS

by Dheepan Ravikumar

The covid outbreak turned the whole world upside down. It is the one among those buses going to run after four months of complete lockdown during the pandemic.

Deva, a dark, tall, and young man somehow managed to get the window seat, no matter what the age is, the craze for the window seats never fades away for him. He was born in a small village nearby Kanchipuram. He studied engineering after getting influenced by some Tamil movies. After a long struggle to find a job for years, he started working as a supervisor for a private firm in Chennai.

It was the last bus to reach Chengalpattu from Kanchipuram. That route was mostly used by farmers, merchants, and villagers. The bus seemed to be very old that reminded of the haunted houses portrayed in Tamil cinemas. The bus started moving slowly, and that's when the Conductor who was standing near the steps, noticed a girl standing with a lot of luggage. The Conductor whistled, and the driver stopped the bus immediately. He asked the girl where she wanted to go. The girl replied, "I want to go to Chennai, but I don't find any bus going to Chennai. So I was looking for a cab or taxi." Conductor explained to her, "Buses won't be entering as the whole city is sealed, there are no taxis or cabs available to reach Chennai from here. Better you get on this bus, and after reaching Chengalpattu, you can go to Chennai." She nodded and agreed as the plan sounded good. Realising the fact that a young, attractive girl was about to enter the bus, people started combing their hair and made sure that they were looking good.

With all her luggage, she managed to get into the bus. It was indeed a difficult task for her. When she was looking for a place to keep her bags, she got distracted entirely with the interior look of the bus. The people inside the bus started mumbling among themselves that she was not really willing to travel on this bus, but she was left with no choice.

The moment she entered the bus, she became the hot topic for passengers to discuss. She was wearing a face mask which was wide enough to hide most of her face. But still, she grabbed the attention of the entire bus.

She was tall, very fair with sharp eyes and raised eyebrows. The attractive earrings were dancing all over her soft, beautiful ears. There was a mole on her forehead, and her curly hair reminded Deva about the girl who acted with Madhavan in a boxing movie, but he wasn't able to guess the movie name though.

As she sat on an individual seat which was parallel to the driver's seat, it made the driver perform some stunts with the steering while driving. She found that the seat was broken, which forced her to sit next to Deva. As a girl like her came closer and sat next to him, Deva could hear his heartbeat now, faster than ever before. He realised that many passengers on the bus might be jealous of him. Since she came back and sat next to Deva, the driver slowed down the bus. So, no more stunts can be expected henceforth.

Deva grew up in a small village, studied in boys only school and college. He was never friends with girls, particularly of his age. He was the kind of person who has been following social distancing very strictly, especially with the girls of his age even before the corona outbreak. The only reason was his shyness.

He didn't want any part of him to bother her. So, he crushed himself towards the window and gave her more space to sit. Later, she got a call, and her loud ringtone conveyed many people on the bus that she was using an iPhone. Deva got to notice the three camera lenses behind the phone and concluded that it was an iPhone 11 which was worth a lakh back then. Deva started smiling within himself when he realised the fact that she was having a phone which was almost the same as his annual income. Then, he moved further away from her and made sure that the space between them was more. She didn't answer the call and disconnected it. And it disappointed many young men on the bus who were very eager to hear her voice.

The way she adjusted her curly hair once every few minutes made everyone crazy. Some ladies in the bus started debating about the price range of her dress. Even though her face was not completely visible, her look and attitude was admired by everyone on the bus. Her fragrance forced Deva to look at her. Having no guts to look at her with a straight face, he was sitting significantly closer to the window, and he was picturing her face inside his head. He became tired of imagining her face and decided that she would look prettier than all the faces he has ever imagined. She must be an angel for sure. Deva said to himself.

Many gossips were going on the bus about her. The ladies inside the bus started discussing that she must be a movie star. Everyone was so curious to look at her face at least once so that they could stop building stories about her. Even the driver never failed to look back at her whenever possible.

After some time, she got another call. She answered this time and started speaking in English, which left everyone in surprise. Deva could barely understand what she was talking, and others weren't able to understand anything. She started speaking louder as her voice was not audible to the person on the other end. It was undeniable that everyone in the bus expected that she would remove her mask while talking. But she didn't. Even the Conductor tried his luck. While giving the ticket to her, he smartly acted as if he couldn't hear her properly. He thought she would remove her mask and speak. But no luck there.

She couldn't help but notice that she was sitting much more comfortably in that two-seater. Because Deva gave her more space by crushing himself towards the window. She felt a bit worried. She understood that he felt uncomfortable while sitting next to her. She was smiling at him. Even though she was wearing the mask, Deva could see her smiling. She said, " hey hi! This is a two-seater, and half of this belongs to you as well. So, sit comfortably". He managed to smile back at her without saying anything.

Meanwhile, she saw a boy selling water bottles nearby the tollgate. She needed Deva's help as he was sitting closer to the window. She asked him, " if you don't mind, could you please get me a water bottle" and gave him a hundred rupee note. Deva felt so happy as if he had achieved something by getting her the water bottle and handing over her balance amount. After watching this, the entire bus thought that she was feeling thirsty. They hoped that she would remove her mask while drinking. Everyone was looking at her very carefully. A few minutes later, she took the bottle and slowly pulled the lid. All of a sudden no one knew what really had happened. She put the lid back and kept the bottle inside her bag. Most of the people in the bus started scolding her like how they used to scold Indian batsman for getting "out for a duck" in run-chase while watching the cricket on TV.

After that, many people realised that she was not going to take her mask. So, the attention towards her got reduced. The Conductor stopped staring at her, and even the driver stopped looking back frequently.

She got a call again. It was her mom, and she was talking in Tamil. It seemed her mother asked her why her voice was tired. She was replying, "Yeah, mom! I am terribly sick and tired. Everything I want now is a strong cup of filter coffee. But I don't think that the bus is going to stop anywhere in the middle." She hung up the phone after a few minutes. Then, she started listening to music with her headphones on. Deva felt terrible that he wasn't able to do anything after knowing that she was not well. Suddenly, the bus was stopped. The Conductor told us there was a breakdown, and it would take half an hour to restart the bus. Almost everyone on the bus, including Deva, got down. Few were helping the Driver and Conductor. Few were relaxing.

Deva saw something on a hoarding board near the bus, he ran back to the bus immediately where she was sitting alone in the bus closing her eyes and listening to music. He didn't know how to get her attention, so he hit her seat gently, which made her open her eyes. Without saying anything, he just pointed his fingers through the window which showed the board that read, "Filter coffees 50 meters ahead." She was surprised by his gesture and thanked him with a smile. She started walking towards that shop alone.

The breakdown was fixed sooner with everyone's help. Deva realised that the bus was going to start soon. He got down from the bus to tell her that the bus was about to leave. While entering the shop, he saw her washing her face, but she didn't notice him. A mirror showed him the whole face. She was left with burns on her nose, cheeks, lips, and shoulder. Deva was stunned, and it was tough to explain how he felt at that moment. He came back to the bus and sat as if nothing had happened. But it was difficult for him to pretend like nothing happened.

She came, and the bus started moving slowly. To break the ice, she asked with a smile, "I know you saw my face completely. I know you saw my face. You got scared. Didn't you?"

"I'm...I'm...really sorry. What happened?"

"Ten years ago, I rejected a guy's proposal. This is what I got. I don't wear a mask, usually. I never had any issue in showing my face. This pandemic forced me to wear this mask. To be honest, this ten-inch cloth gave me those ten years back. I really enjoyed it when everyone on the bus started admiring me, and I didn't want to disappoint them by removing this mask." She ended with a heavenly smile. Deva was broken, and he didn't know what to reply.

"Hey! Stop that! I can even tolerate another acid attack but not sympathies. Thanks for helping me to get my coffee. After the acid attack, everyone started treating me differently except my cup of coffee. It treated me the same all these years without any sympathy. You got to see my face only because of my addiction to coffee. For me, having coffee is like taking selfies. No matter how broken and burnt I'm, the coffee has always forced me to smile, or I ended up pretending that I'm smiling. I'll always have coffee no matter how worse my life gets. It gives me the hope which this society failed to give me."

Deva couldn't stop smiling after listening to her story with that heavenly laugh of hers. He started gazing at her blushing beauty and realised how our sympathies would hurt others. The bus reached its destination, and a car was already waiting for her. Before she got into the car, she winked her eyes and said goodbye to Deva.

Deva was pleased with her gesture and shook his head while waving his hands. The car started moving, and soon it vanished away from his sight. He took a cigarette out from his pocket and lit it. He had few puffs and said to himself, ***"What I imagined is right. She is indeed an angel, but she is far beautiful than the faces I imagined for her."***

Ever since that day, every haunted, broken bus and coffee shops reminded him of her.

19

COFFEE, LUST, LOVE

by Karthick A

Sir, order please?”

“One Toffee Cappuccino’”

“Regular or king, sir?”

“King, please!”

It was a wonderful evening. Cloudy, yet drizzling. I took two chairs-table setups near the window. I felt the dark brown chair over the corner talking to me. The unveiled paint reflected a state of solitary. It said to me, “You are all alone it seems, like me”. But I was not alone. I had a book with me and some stationary partners - an HB pencil dark enough to make an impression in notes taking and a pink highlighter which I use to scribble and spot some essential keywords, especially if it is a non-fiction book. Learning new jargon is funny. Coffee, rain, window seat, and book - a perfect blend for any bibliophile to create his world of ecstasy, at least for that moment, I replied to it with a cunning smirk that I was not alone. I never was. I never will be.

“Sir, Your Toffee Cappuccino.”

“Thank you!”

I was about to drink. And there she entered the shop. She was opening the door slowly, and her multi-colour shiny bangles were making a calm rhythm matching with the jingle bells hanging on the door. She was smiling at me with a surprise. Her both eyebrows were waving higher symmetrically at me, pulling my heart towards her like the effect of the moon's gravity on tidal waves. Her smile was like the sun rays passing through the drizzling rain droplets. She was like a rainbow. Believe me; I was jaw-dropping.

I had a dream the other day that I proposed to her at this same coffee shop. She was about to reply to me. But the alarm clock sound which never bothered me all these days collapsed that very moment. The last thing I saw in my dream was her smile - the same smile, which I was seeing in person.

"Hi, Siddharth", she said.

"Hi, Meera", I was gazing at her dazzling brown eyes, and glossy pink rose lips. Both were poetic. I wanted to gaze at her for my whole eternal life.

"Meeting her was a coincidence or what? I wanted to propose to her for a long time. But I couldn't. Can I seize this moment? To let my dream become a reality. Will she accept my proposal?

I decided not to waste this wonderful moment, and I am going to propose to her. There is an anonymous saying that 'The best relationship usually begins unexpectedly'. Let it begin now!" I was talking to myself until she came towards me and asked, "Can I sit here?".

Then, that same brown chair in solitary minutes ago was not alone anymore, and it was giving me a devilish impression. I am jealous at that moment.

"It's a surprise, and I am happy to see you after a long while, Meera. How are you?"

"I am not surprised at all, But I am happy. I am doing great. How are you? I was planning to meet you soon after reaching my hometown.

I expected you would be at the bookstore. But you are here at Coffee day. What a coincidence!"

"It's drizzling, so I thought to have a cup of cappuccino before I visit the bookstore."

"Toffee's my favourite!"

I whispered, "I know sweetheart."

"Let me order one, Wait a minute."

"You can have it. It's a KING'S one."

"Well, let me taste a bit of it."

"Yes! Please." Her lipstick was all over the straw.

"Wow! Yummy". She gave it back. The straw was back. I took a sip of cappuccino. Technically, I kissed her, and I tasted her soft rose petal lips, but with Toffee flavour.

"So, what is your current reading now?"

"It's a non-fiction book called 'Why we sleep' - about sleep and its importance. I have not been sleeping at all. I have been trying to find a better book to know about sleep deprivation and how it affects our health. Ironically, I drink coffee to overcome my sleep sometimes just for the sake of completing the crime thriller novels, which were under hibernation for a long while."

"Ha-ha! Hope you follow the technique from that book and have a good sleep after reading, I hope. Don't forget to teach me later as usual you do."

"I wish to. But I don't think I would sleep peacefully anymore."

"Why so?"

"Can I tell her now? Absolutely Yes. No more delay. I am going to propose to her." I was whispering to my heart.

Suddenly, I stopped worrying about everything and told her, "Because of you."

"Uh?" she reacted in a way as if she already knew that I was going to propose.

"Yes, Because of you. You don't let me sleep peacefully. I thought my circadian rhythm and sleep pattern is disturbed by late-night coffee and an increase in adenosine. But It is you always. Science says Caffeine has a half-life of 7 hours, that it takes 50% of it to flush out from the human body, remaining 50% still accumulates. But you are way more powerful drug than Caffeine. You are my drug—your eyes, lips, smile. Everything shatters my entire nervous system. Every neuron of my brain stops communicating with each other through an electric signal after gazing at you. My whole body is shut down because of you."

She was in awe and speechless.

"I am in love with you. You have done enough damage to me. When I see you every time in my dream and reality, my adrenaline spikes, my heart races, my pupil dilates".

"Haan...What?" she was still in awe.

"High level of Dopamine Meera. I couldn't sleep, I couldn't eat—the intense rush of pleasure. You are playing with my serotonin - Love's most important chemical. My whole thinking is always about you."

"You are clever and sweet enough to make me fall for you Siddharth."

"Is it?"

"Well! I think she already fell." I started whispering to my heart. I was bugging my facial muscles to smile in a way to show it was witty and cunning.

"You should stop doing that!" Meera intervened.

"Doing what? Drinking Coffee or Reading books? Or..looking at you???" I smirked

"Nooooooo! You should stop whispering and talking to yourself. You could tell me anything! I mean we could talk about anything."

I said, "You know Meera? Two more hormones yet to play its major role. Oxytocin, a powerful hormone which releases during sex and orgasm. Vasopressin, which releases after sex. It's symbolic of long-term commitment."

That was it. I had done my part.

"That's too much science, but this is...", she laughed.

"Do you love me, Meera?"

"I like the way you expressed it. But will you be quite poetic? I will tell you then."

"Like how?" I asked.

I could feel that she held her breath for a moment. 'I will text you. I got to go now', she smiled, winked, and left.

I can't believe I proposed to her and recalled all the drama that happened late in the evening over a cup of coffee. It was 9 pm. I was on my bed with my book. I had been waiting for her text, biting my nail out of curiosity about what she was going to tell.

A few minutes later, I received a text from her – "Check Michael Faudet's 'Teach me'. That is my answer to you."

I searched the poem on google.

TEACH ME

Such pretty things

you said to me –

Unbutton me

some more

For I am yours

to take tonight

upon this forest floor

Let's make a bed

in autumn leaves,

and leave

no leaf turned

Beneath these trees

please teach me,

please –

To learn

a love

unlearned

Another message notification – "I already fell in love with you. Your proposal came with an expiry date today."

Her estrogen vanquished my testosterone heavily. She won!

Next text followed - "Try to write one poem for me. Dare to beat me with your words. There is no coffee without love. There is no love without lust."

"There is no love without lust." She was right. It reminded me about a poem (not exactly!) I wrote for her a long time back. It was time to send my lust missile.

'*That Soulmate Thing*'

Your Nudity is the mirror of my divine soul, Enlightening.

Your Virginity is the shade of my preserved lust. Gratifying.

All my ten hardhat electrified fingers are excited to light your one-way dark road path inside your dry perforated cotton threads'.

She replied with full of red hearts and a flying kiss emojis. I replied to her, "It is going to be another sleepless night. I don't need coffee anymore."

She sent a reply immediately, "Are you sure about the coffee part? Like, for real??? Because I might need one right now. Also, I am on the way to Madras Coffee house."

"You might also need a company! So, your boyfriend is coming." I typed the message quickly and started my bike.

That Day! That King Toffee Cappuccino! That crazy conversation has changed my life forever.

20

THE MEMORIE CLUB

by Shaymi Shah

It was the night all the members of the club had been waiting for. It was the night where some of the most important decisions were going to be made. Everyone wanted to know who was going to win the awards this year. This was the most awaited event of the year. All the nominees had worked very hard all year.

There were so many among them who had been nominated almost every year but never got the award. Most of them would get disappointed upon hearing the results, but some were so optimistic that they would take it as an opportunity to work harder and try the next year again.

This event was hosted by the "Memorie Club" every year, and Kiara Sharma was the founder of this club. She was full of ideas to make sure that the way this club worked was unique and different. First of all, anyone who entered the club was considered to be a member. Secondly, since it was a free entry- the only thing the members were expected to do was to make sure they participate in the activities that happened here all year, analyse their learnings from the activities, and submit a progress report at the end of the year. It would help the committee to decide who would be getting nominated for the annual recognition awards.

The categories for nominations in this particular award function was different from other clubs. This year was the 25th Anniversary of this club, so she had decided to go about the award-giving the process a little differently. It was going to be a surprise for all the members- everyone was going to be a winner in some or the other way.

The event started at 7 o'clock with a presentation- to give a glimpse to the audience about everything that had happened in the club celebrating the 25 years of happiness and pride. It was going to be an evening full of surprises, excitement, and celebration.

Soon the presentation got over, and the anchor came on stage to tell the audience about how they had planned this evening for them. It was going to begin by revealing some of the most important awards and end with a tribute to one of the most important members of this club for their life-long dedication in working for the progress of this club.

The anchor started by announcing the first category of nominations - the best comic. Two nominations were shortlisted in this category, after a lot of confusion, as there were just so many options to choose from.

1) Midnight coffee- The roommates had been working all evening, and at around three in the night they took a coffee break. They had been working non-stop as they were both very stressed out to finish the submission for the next morning. They decided to watch some funny videos from the movies they liked and laughed for almost an hour before they got back to work again.

2) Midday coffee- The daughter came home from her college after a long time. She, her mother, and her sister had all gone to their favourite coffee place in the city, and in a rush, she forgot there was some coffee left in her sister's glass and put her glass in it, thereby spilling it in the car. They all laughed it off and drove back home, calling it "Her new normal". They had come to terms with the fact that she was a soon-to-be architect, and this is one of the most "normal"

things one can expect from her- they had heard crazier stories about aspiring architects her age.

The anchor invited Miss Kiara to give away the award. She soon announced that the winner was the "midnight coffee" as it still made her laugh just the same whenever she thought about it. The midday coffee, though, was to be given a prize of being cherished consistently.

The next anchor came on stage to announce the second category of nominations- the best narrative. Three nominations were shortlisted as follows:

1) Existential Theories- Four friends from college had reunited after a long time and gone to the new cafe in town. While the three of them had ordered cheesecake, the most impulsive one had ordered a cold brew just to try something new. Their conversation soon turned into a debate- the question being- if humans as a species didn't exist, would all the other species be able to live peacefully on this planet? The evening light slowly faded into the night as hours passed by, but their conversation only seemed to make them feel more alive.

2) Before Sunrise- The five best friends met every time she came back for the weekend at home. They were all so different from each other, but it was the similarities in their differences that had made their bond grow only stronger with time. They would all gather at her place, post-dinner, catch up for all the time they were away, make Maggie and coffee at midnight- a tradition since school time and watch a movie later. While three of them would sleep off eventually, the rest of the two would be up till sunrise talking about life, maturing, and evolving into the beautiful women that they had grown into.

3) After Sunset- She would take her brothers and sister out for a drive- going around the city, exploring different parts of it, with their favourite music playing in the background of their non-stop conversations and sometimes stop by their favourite coffee shop- they called it their "adda". One such time they found a place, a little farther away from the airport where, if they waited just enough, they could see the aeroplane go so closely from above them right before landing on

the runway. They debated if that could become their new adda but eventually, they all agreed that the coffee place remained at the top.

The anchor asked Kiara to give away the award. She soon announced that the winner was "Before Sunrise" because it was something that had managed to remain consistently the same, and was a full-proof example of how their bond had strengthened over time. The other two nominations, though, were to be given a prize of becoming translated into visual stories that would be released across all the other clubs and get a virtual recognition.

The anchor came on stage to announce the third category of nominations- the best supporting role. Two nominations were shortlisted as follows:

1) Perfect Mismatch- She was a coffee person, and he- a tea lover. But somehow her love for coffee made him start liking it as well. Her love for the evening light, made him fall in love with it just as much as he loved the moonlit sky at night. Moreover, his love for the smell of wet sand after the rain started mesmerizing her. While realizing how they shared similar interests but not the same, what they also realised is how deeply they had fallen in love with each other. Unknowingly, they had become the perfect mismatch and eventually a lifelong support system for each other.

2) Invincible Duo- They always had a debate about whether he was more of a friend to him than a father or not. They had this telepathic connection, a bond so strong, people around them couldn't believe existed. Whether it was a long drive around the city with him giving her advice about how to deal with life or just sitting on the swings in the evening, having a cup of coffee, teaming up with her to tease her little sister. He was a guardian, a father, and most of all, a friend who translated her thoughts into words.

The anchor asked Kiara to give away the award. She soon announced that the winner was surprisingly a tie between the two nominations. It was the first time something like this had happened, but the decision was so hard to make that she had decided to award both the nominees. Both were called up on stage and given a huge round of applause. In addition to virtual recognition, these two nominees would also be given the title of the most precious members of the club and provided exclusive benefits.

The anchor announced that it was time for yet another performance before they went on with the award ceremony. It was going to be a storytelling performance by Miss Kiara Sharma. It was one of the most awaited performances of this event as she was going to reveal a few secrets through her stories about how this club was formed years ago.

The audience was dumbstruck at the end of the story to know that they were the story- they were the ones who had already formed an identity by simply existing. They didn't know that Miss Sharma was merely the one who gave this identity a name and eventually formed a club to give all of them a much-deserved focus. The audience was so amazed at the idea that they gave her a standing ovation.

Once everyone settled back in their seats, the anchor came on stage again to announce the final award of the event. This Lifetime achievement award gave recognition to the member who had dedicatedly worked towards the progress of the club. Miss Kiara was called on-stage again to announce the winner.

She smiled when she opened the card on which the name was written and decided to first give a short description of him before revealing the name of the winner. She began, "He had worked day and night, to make sure every member was given certain importance once they entered the Memorie club. He had also helped in uplifting the spirits of the ones who felt undermined and overwhelmed upon entering the club, felt lost or demotivated. He had made sure they got a place to stay, even if he felt overburdened. He wasn't the one to let go of any of the members easily. He was a brave fighter who would go against all odds to protect all the members. There were so many times that the club was under threat from the members of the other clubs who were their rivals, but he was the one who had stood unshaken in every circumstance to make sure everything remained in order.

I now call the winner of the "Lifetime Achievement Award", he is the one who has made sure all the members (the memories) live here happily. Ladies and Gentlemen, Please welcome

"The Subconscious Mind" on stage. I am so happy to be giving away this award to someone so dear to me. The best thing about him is how he made sure that all my favourite members (memories- especially of experiences and stories revolving around coffee) were safe and secure.

The announcement followed a huge round of applause and a standing ovation.

21

LUCILLE AT THE AUCTION

by Peter Jewkes

London

A damp Friday

Lucille Melting was doing just that, melting with worry. She was in her palatial office concerned about the company she worked for – Comco.

She loved her coffee, but it wasn't making her feel much better.

Comco was on the slide, however fitful or temporary the fall from grace was. For some reason, which was, for the present, inexplicable, targets weren't being met, and two consecutive sets of quarterly figures had been below city and industry expectations. New products had not come to market with anything like proper speed, and competitors were stealing a march at each and every opportunity. Comco didn't do falls in sales, or at least never had before.

Lucille had joined nearly two years ago at the crest of the wave, a golden girl, headhunted, lunched, and finally captured with a golden handshake and a golden set of share options that were now rapidly going down the golden toilet.

Heads were due to roll, and Lucille's was one of those on the block.

Consequently, and for the first time in her life, work was a worry. The only way Lucille had found to combat that kind of anxiety was to work ever harder to batter problems into submission. The evening so far had seen her becoming increasingly round-shouldered as she crouched in front of her computer trying every which way to arrive at a plausible explanation for the dramatic fall-off in sales. Caught in a whirl of projections, programmes, budgets, minutes of management meetings and the cold shoulder of what really happened, time disappeared until...

'9 o'clock, more coffee.'

Then it dawned on her that she was late for the party.

Lucille had a thing about punctuality. Emerson had phoned a couple of weeks ago to invite, or, rather, beg her to come to a party he was having at his now ancient loft apartment in what had once been a fashionable area of old London docklands. She had said yes because he had cried on the phone, desperate, he had said, for support.

"What the hell kind of a party is this, Emerson?"

"The worst kind. It's my divorce party. And even more than the worst because all of her friends will be there and I'm not sure I'll have anyone!"

"OK, you can count on me. What time?"

"Please be there by 9.30. Please. Please."

"OK, OK. Don't go on so. And for God's sake, don't snivel when I get there."

She hadn't yet changed for the event but needed to get on the road. She was brought to reality by her secretary returning from a shopping trip with black tights, red lipstick, and a curt reminder that enough overtime was enough when you had a weekend ahead that was there to enjoy.

Lucille ran down the stairs clutching the clothes.

Out onto the wet street.

"TAXI!!!"

In the cab:

"OK, moron, just keep your eyes on the road, and we'll get along just fine."

"Yes, miss."

"And don't 'miss' me. OK?" (Shouting now)

"No, miss."

Lucille was having to work hard to make these words carry with their intended weight, having taken up a prone position on the back seat of the cab with her legs raised high enough to enable her to slip the new pair of black tights up to her waist. More than that, she was very tired and very irritable.

Why the hell hadn't she changed at the office?

A light rain was making the roads greasy as the cab slid over Tower Bridge. At the same time, Lucille zipped up her very small black dress, panting from her considerable exertions in such a small space. A few minutes later and the warehouse appeared on their right, and the cabby halted his livelihood, clicked off the meter and took the eight pounds as if giving change was akin to criminal behaviour.

"Thanks, miss."

"Yeah, stuff you too."

The front door was ajar for the party and was guarded by a large man with no hair and an even larger woman.

Lucille remembered.

This marriage had broken up because Virginia, a previously ardent exponent of all matters pertaining to the physical delights of heterosexuality, had been led to even greater heights of passion and political fulfilment by an interesting blonde professor on a weekend course who just happened to be a woman.

Her mentality suitably adjusted for the better, Virginia had sued for divorce and had been encouraged by her new allies to ensure maximum levels of acrimony. All assets were to be sold, including the flat, but before that finally went, there was a demand from her side that all contentious items be placed there and be subject to an ownership debate at a party to which the friends and allies of both sides be invited.

The lift arrived and opened its creaking doors. Like many lifts in these kinds of buildings, it was a leftover from industrial days and consequently could take about fifty people or bales of cotton but only travel at the rate of one floor every minute or so.

Lucille persevered. As the lift groaned higher (she was destined for the fifth and top floor) the sound of the ownership debate grew louder and seemed to be in full swing. She felt herself growing smaller.

The doors up here were wide open, and the exposed brickwork of the main walls became visible. There was a lot of noise.

"Hi, there! Welcome to the party! I am one of your servers for tonight, and my name is Darren."

"Thanks!"

"Bride or groom?"

"Groom, I guess."

"Over to the right then please."

Lucille walked into the room with as much dignity as she could muster and immediately regretted wearing the little black number. To the right-hand end of the one-hundred-foot main space, Emerson had made the gross error of insisting that most of his guests wear the same clothes as on the day of his wedding. Grey toppers, grey suits, red carnations. Great taste.

To the left, the floor seethed with girls in lilac leather expecting an 'On the Waterfront' evening.

Bars either end of the room were manned and womanned by agency staff. Mostly university students and lacking the savoir-faire associated with the young communists of the 1960s, clad in traditional black and white, their initial bemusement was slowly turning to horror, a horror that would later render them so terrified as to leave without wages, forgetting to fill their pockets with the perks of a normal evening.

In the centre lay the goodies. Two refectory tables carried the sorry remnants of Virginia and Emerson's' divorce procedures, articles that lay in dispute not because either party really wanted them but because neither could bear to give another inch.

The music was suddenly cut to a scratching stop. George Ingledale, the best man at the accursed wedding, had become drunk enough to have a good idea. Grabbing a chair, he rose ceilingward, supported only by three chums from the rowing club.

"Sounds daft, but I've had a great idea."

"First one ever then."

"No, really, I think this will be damned good."

"What are you waiting for?"

"Get on with it!"

"OK, OK. Here it is then. This stuff all looks like a load of complete crap to me. Please don't let's wait for no one to want it. Let's auction it all. Proceeds to go towards some cases of champagne from around the corner."

"Who's in charge?"

"Me and one of you, or no go."

"Done!"

Discussions in a huddle produced a svelte lilac leather girl from Hounslow as the gay auctioneer. Not the bride, for Virginia had taken up a throne in the far back corner, high on a packing case where she could survey her once photographed and published domain. Thin smoke from her cigar curled towards the detectors whose efficacy had been throttled by the simple means of removing the batteries.

She was enjoying herself, her professor long gone, but surrounded by recent and latent amusements.

The auctioneers were perilously balanced on hire chairs, each supported by a volunteer from the expectant ranks below.

George was losing his presence of mind

"Lot number one is this delightful, embroidered portrait of Richard Nixon, designed, executed and sent as a birthday present to Emerson by an ailing American aunt shortly before Watergate."

"What am I bid?"

"2p"

"5p"

"Come on you toerags, this is an amazingly prescient item, wooled with care and love for the man. Let's see a decent bid!"

"10p"

"OK, I'll give you a quid."

"Two"

"How much is the champagne?"

"About fifteen quid, I think."

"All right then, fifteen, I'm getting a massive thirst."

"Sold to the lady in lilac."

Massive applause greeted this most sensible of bids. The DJ scratched a salvo of edges, rising to an unbearable crescendo before descending to a burped version of Madonna's low notes in Medium Track Woman.

George wobbled. No one thought to steady him.

"Thank you. Thank you. Thank you! The next item is a miniature china dachshund made in Taiwan. I have no further provenance."

Lucille parted company with the auction and moved to the bar at the back of the groom's area. The floor was already as wet as the streets outside but smelled powerfully of a heady concoction of beer and wine.

"I'll take a Kummel,' she said, spotting the half-empty bottle beneath a pile of crisp packets, 'In fact, I think I'll take it all."

"Certainly, Madam"

She looked for Emerson. She espied him, like Claudius, ensconced on a low dais, weeping into his San Miguel, comforted by a redhead with dazzling teeth who clearly had designs on him and his future fortunes. He waved a weak and cod like hand to Lucille before ignoring her in the redhead's neck. No matter, the man was taken care of.

Lucille raised the bottle to her lips and took a decent swig. The sweet stuff trickled down and straight away began to remove her hurting head and some of her worries. She had started the thought that God, is this how it is for everyone, I should drink more often when a dispute arose at the auction. George, labouring under the misapprehension that they were desirable only to a certain section of the population, had knocked down the sale of a packet of unused Jamaican condoms (full size) to a senior member of the groom's party when the lilac auctioneer protested that a better bid had come in from a lilac member whose total commitment to the cause was a little uncertain.

Afterwards, no one could remember who had thrown the first punch or broken the first chair over someone else's head. All Lucille knew was that the room was suddenly mayhem, the air a dangerous place full of flying objects and eye level a good place for a knuckle sandwich.

She saw blood, but not her own.

Dropping to all fours, she scurried towards what she thought was the door, opened it and crept inside, only to find herself the second occupant of the cleaning cupboard, now made roomy by the removal of the contents by equal measure to the new abodes of the bride and groom.

"Hello."

"Hello!"

"Come here often?"

"Have done, but probably not again."

Something heavy thudded against the door. It groaned, scuffled, and departed.

"Chin Har Tan"

"Is it really? I'm so sorry. Can I help?"

"No, no, that's my name."

"For God's sake, no more surprises. How do you spell that? I can only pronounce strange things if I can see them written down."

"C-H-I-N H-A-R- T-A-N"

"Thanks. What do I call you?"

"Chin will do."

"OK, Chin. Sorry. My name is Lucille. Lucille Melting."

"Hello, Lucille"

The heavy thing thudded again and stayed there without scuffling or groaning.

Lucille squirmed around and tried to find a place to sit.

"Lookout, watch where you're going."

"Sorry, what am I doing wrong?"

"You're trying to sit on my auction purchase."

"Sorry, what is it?"

"Well, I went crazy the other day and bought a 500 quid coffee maker, and when I saw these cups, I knew I had to have them."

"Let's have a look then."

Lucille burrowed into the Sainsburys carrier bag and brought out a paper-covered parcel. She unwrapped it to find the most beautiful, almost transparent, porcelain cups and saucers, the cups tiny and hemispherical, the saucers almost flat with a delicate indent.

"They ARE fabulous."

"Five cups and six saucers, unfortunately, but good enough for me."

"I'd kill for a cup of good coffee right now. And I seem to have kept this bottle of Kummel."

"Your place or mine?"

"We'll go where the machine is, don't you think?"

Lucille and Chin were making their way down the escape stairs and out of the fire doors as the police were commandeering the lift and the front entrance ready to brighten their Friday evening with a few politically unsound arrests.

"TAXI!!!!!"

22

THE JOY OF PROCAFFEINATING

by Prerna Agrawal

Procaffeinating means the tendency of not to start anything until you've had a cup of coffee. The word "Procaffeinating" would mean "me" in the dictionary.

My day starts with a coffee and ends with a coffee. I have one cup of coffee each morning to start the day off right. The other ones are to keep me out of the mess in my life a bit, help me to deal with my problems and fuel my energy. I am sure you also drink lots of coffee if you're a coffee lover like me.

One day, I woke up and saw the calendar, the day was circled with a red marker pen, and the cake was waiting for me. Yes, It was my birthday. There was a grand party at my home. All my relatives were there, and I had a great day, probably the best birthday in a long time. At night around 11 pm, it started to rain. I was standing in my balcony. "What about a cup of coffee, at night with this lovely weather? " a voice came from behind.

Yes, it was my lovely mom. "How do you know I wanted that," I asked her with a surprise.

"Dear, I am your mom, I know everything about you, what do you need at what time" She came towards me. "I love you so much," I replied and leaned on her shoulder. "I know, and I love you too. Now come on drink this coffee and go off to bed, it's too late. You need to get up early tomorrow, " she finished saying and gave me a good night kiss. "Yes, good night, mom", I replied and then she left the room. Coffee is a cup of hope in a world full of chaos and mess, and it is my partner. I was enjoying the lovely weather with my coffee. Then suddenly, a thought struck my mind. "How about starting a job as a writer? " I asked myself.

I came inside my room, sat on my chair, took out a diary and a pen and started to write. That day I slept at 4 am. "Get up, sweetheart, you need to go for a job interview." My mom woke me up by saying this at 8 am. I had finished my B.A and was looking for a job as an editor at one of the newspaper companies. "Five more minutes, mom! Please!!!" I replied. "No, Dear! Get up otherwise you will be late for the interview and here is your coffee, drink and get ready fast, till then I am making breakfast for you," she said to me and left the room.

I got up, brushed my teeth, sat down on my bed to drink my coffee. I don't drink coffee to wake up; I wake up to drink coffee. A few minutes later, my eyes went to my diary, which I wrote the other night. I opened the journal and read my story, "It's a quite good story! Shit!!!! It's 9 am. I need to get ready faster. Otherwise, I will miss the interview," I told myself, and I rushed to my bathroom. At 9:30 am, I came downstairs to have my breakfast. "Come, I was waiting for you only. Here is your breakfast", my mom was relieved. How about Allu paratha with pickle and scrambled egg, served with mom's love? Nothing can be better than that for me, especially when it's filled with mom's love. I had my breakfast and left for the interview. I was there at the office by 10 am. Thank God, I was on time. I was sitting in the waiting room with lots of hope and excitement.

"Prerna Agrawal, you're being called for the interview, please go to room no. 4," the lady called me. I got up and went for my interview. After fifteen minutes, I came back from the interview and sat down on my seat. I was waiting for the result. Around 2 pm, the lady came and announced the names of selected candidates. A wide smile appeared on my face when I heard my name. I went and filled the rest of the forms, and I was informed to join the office from next month. I came back home with a big smile on my face. "Mom, I got the job," I was jumping and hugged her. A big smile appeared on her face after hearing the news. She looked even prettier with that sweet smile of hers. She made Halwa for me with lots of love. After having my favourite halwa, I went back to my room. I changed and sat down on my bed. I opened that diary again and started writing with a cup of coffee I drank hell a lot of coffee while writing, which helped me to stay awake and think of a new idea so that I could finish my book. Number of coffees I had while writing is higher than the number of drafts I wrote for my book. Within a month, I finished writing the book.

I was writing the book all day and night. I thought of publishing my book, and on the other hand, I was also doing my job. I tried many places for publishing my book, but I got rejected everywhere. I wrote another book, and that got rejected as well. After every rejection, I used to sit with a cup of coffee to release my stress, and it helped me to think of new ideas, and I finished another book with a new and a fresh idea. I used to drink more than two to three cups of coffee while writing my book.

One night I got a call from my best friend, Kirti. "Hey, bro! How are you?" she asked me. "I am good. what about you?". "I am good too," she said and continued, "Bro, it's been so long! Let's meet tomorrow. I am here in Kolkata and even Ankit he is here, " I was super excited already. "Yeah, sure. Tomorrow at the 4 pm coffee shop," I told, and she agreed for the location. We talked for an hour, and then I checked my phone, it was around 1 am, I had to sleep.

The next day I went to meet them. They were already there. We ordered three cups of coffee. "Remember how we used to bunk our classes just to come here for having coffee," I exclaimed. "Yeah, just because of you. You love drinking coffee, and you used to bring us here for literally everything" Kirti smirked. "Haha. Yes! Coffee is LIFE " I bragged and continued, "Coffee is my love. It's not just a cup of coffee. It's a cup full of memories. Our life is also like a cup of coffee.

Sometimes the taste of coffee is good, and sometimes it's bad, our days of life are also the same, some days are bad, and some days are good, but we must not forget to enjoy it, whether it's coffee or our days of life." At the very moment, something struck me, and then I shrieked with excitement, "I got an idea". My friends got confused and gushed" Idea??? What???? What Idea???". "Guess what! I can write a book on coffee. Coffee has been my partner in my good and bad days, and there are many things I can say about coffee in my book. Coffee has given me unrealistic expectations and productivity". My friends started screaming, and Kirti added, "That's awesome! OMG!!! You should write a book about it! Trust me. Your book will get published this time", and then she called for a group hug. We were talking for an hour, then we left. I came back home, had my dinner, and went back to my room.

I took out my diary, a pen and sat down to write my new book with a cup of coffee. "It all started with a cup of coffee". That was the title I fixed for my book. Whenever I had to write for my book, I always needed a cup of coffee. That one cup of coffee kept me awake and helped me to explore various ideas for my book. I had a lot of coffee when I was writing my book. It took me almost a year to finish writing. With the help of my coffee and my ideas, I was able to finish my book. I tried a few places to publish that book, and with God's grace, it got published. I was so happy to have my book. It seemed like my dream has come true. That day was an unforgettable day for me because I was going to read my book with my favourite cup of coffee in front of a large audience.

I wore my favourite red dress with white sneakers. I left my home much earlier so that I can be on time, but I didn't know that day will change my life forever. The right side of my car, where I was sitting, took a direct hit with a bus. I was covered with blood. They took me to the hospital, and after seeing me, the doctor informed my parents that there were significantly fewer chances for me to survive. For months, my treatment was going on, and one day finally, I opened my eyes. My mom's eyes were filled with happy tears when she saw me. The doctor told me that I would never be able to walk again. Yes, I was paralysed, but I never gave up on writing. Finally, I was home after a long time. I sat with my favourite cup of coffee and started writing my grief, my pain, my emotions. I don't know if writers are cursed or blessed because even their grief becomes an inspiration to write, and when it's with a cup of coffee, it turns out to be amazing.

I just want to say that close your eyes and imagine the best version of you possible. That's who you really are. Let go of any part of you that doesn't believe it. Your spirit needs recharging at least as often as your phone or laptop. Make time to reconnect with yourself. Just for today sit and sip a cup of coffee, forget your trouble a little bit, ignore the tasks you have to do and enjoy a cup or two.

23

WHEN ONLY LOVE EXISTS

by Suganya Kumar

In our modern age, there are so many ways for information to travel. And yet with all those smartphones, iPads, Tablets, there are still some people who like to get their morning newspaper from a local shop, make a cup of strong coffee for themselves, and take their beautiful journal note and write something. Sarah is one of them. She is an English Professor who absolutely loves writing something about everything. Sarah never missed any chance when it comes to exploring her writing skills. No matter how busy she is, she always finds time for the things she loves the most.

Exactly a year ago when she was scrolling through her newsfeed on Instagram. She found an "Open Mic" online contest where people can participate from their own place. Participants have to record video at their home and send it to them. Shortlisted participants will be asked to present their content in the virtual open Mic meet, which happens via Zoom call. The theme was "A lot can happen over a cup of coffee". Little did Sarah know that's how she was going to meet "The One". Only five got shortlisted for the finals, Sarah and Karthik were among those five.

Karthik is an aspiring director who has directed many short films and is waiting for his feature film release. His parents died in an accident when he was seven years old. He grew up in an orphanage. So, he ended up spending most of his childhood days reading or writing on a paper about the favourite characters he has read, what they were like, how they are all connected. He knows more about the characters in the book than the people in his life. Ever since then, every person he meets, every wandering road he takes, every place, every destination, every sound he listens to, are added to the story of his life. Everything in life is a source of artistic influence for him. In his eyes, everything is a living, breathing work of art that he could interpret and write in every possible way. Karthik fell for Sarah when she told "Coffee is her muse". He is a hollow shell without his black coffee. Coffee has always been his muse until he met her.

That was not "Love at first sight". It was "Love at First Word".

They never realised that love could happen so fast. Karthik fell for her hidden metaphors, and Sarah fell for his storytelling. But they haven't confessed yet. Soon after the contest, they exchanged their Instagram id's and started talking on Instagram. Their conversation started like coffee lovers, later they ended up becoming lovers. After three months of texting and video calls, they finally decided to meet at "Café Coffee day" which is significantly closer to the Marina beach. As their first virtual meet happened over a coffee and with café Coffee day's logo, they wanted their actual meet to also occur at the same place.

Sarah looked like an angel in her white salwar kameez. The Kajal, in her eyes, made her look even more beautiful. Her palms were sweating. She was feeling strange, different, and happy. Because that was their first meet. She was waiting for Karthik, whose face was very familiar to her with all the zoom meetings and skype calls they had over the past few months. Karthik was wearing a black shirt and came towards her. Sarah sighed and smiled in relief.

"Salwar kameez looks good on you," he said, and he couldn't take his eyes off her.

"Don't I look good on Salwar kameez?" Sarah was furious.

"Come on! I don't want to do this. You were terrific in the 1920*1080 pixels. If I were one among those pixels, I would have written 1000 poems about you."

She threw him a reproving glance and asked, "Just 1000?"

"We are not doing this now! Let's have our coffee." Karthik took her to one of his favourite spot in the café and ordered their favourite coffees. At the beach, time doesn't move hour to hour but mood to the moment. There is nothing more beautiful than the waves that refuse to stop. Just like those waves, both were denying their feelings they have for each other. They were holding their coffee cups with each other aside. Rainy days were made for drinking coffee, and that day was made for them. No matter how many times the waves are sent away, but they would always come again to kiss the shoreline. That's how human feelings are! The more you refuse, the more you feel.

She is an English Professor, and he is a director. It is the rarest and yet beautiful combination in the world. They were talking about literature, movies, books, and series, everything except their feelings for each other. With every sip of coffee, they were Inhaling the aroma of coffee and exhaling their feelings. That beautiful evening added a lot of beautiful moments in their life.

They started hanging out often. Karthik was living alone. The care and the love Sarah showed to him was comforting. He was drenched in her love. Their day always ended with a cup of coffee. Karthik showed a lot of respect for her feelings and emotions. We cannot choose who we love. But we can choose how we love them. And some people can only show love by respecting your feelings and choices. Karthik is one among them.

It's been a year now since they started talking, and in two days, it will be Sarah's first birthday with him. He planned a big surprise for her birthday. He took her to the beach where they met for the first time.

Nothing says birthday like lights and balloons! No cake is better than a Coffee bean custom cake for a coffee lover! There is nothing more romantic than roses and candles! Things that cannot be expressed in words are better done with music! How would it be when the entire crowd is dancing for your favourite song! How would it be when he sweeps her away from the monotonous daily life and surprises her by taking her on a boat ride! That's how the love of her love surprised her. On the middle of the beach, she saw another ship coming towards them. It had a huge banner hanging off the side that reads "Sarah, are you ready to listen to my stories forever." She started crying after reading those words and turned back. He got down on one knee, and she said "Yes". She didn't even let him speak. That was the moment they are going to remember till eternity.

The proposal was even better than anything she could have imagined, or she could have read in any literature books. Her favourite place, her favourite music, and a perfect ring that he has chosen without any of her inputs! That was her best birthday to date. Almost exactly a week later, the unexpected global pandemic happened.

The Indefinite Lockdown was announced everywhere. Everyone was forced to stay inside the home, and it was called "new normal". What is normal if you can't be with the one you love the most? Karthik and Sarah started missing each other, yet they stayed connected virtually.

Months were passing, and it was getting worse every day. The indefinite lockdown developed a strange fear among everyone. They were struggling to adapt to the new normal. But they made sure that their last call for the day ended with their virtual coffee date. Days were passing, and they started fighting for the smallest of things. The COVID-19 has affected every aspect of their life. Both wanted to meet each other, but they couldn't. Even though they were living in the same city, it felt like they were in different continents. But coffee was a connecting bridge between them. They were just one cup away from a totally different reality.

They believed that the universe would make the people get back with their loved ones soon. The existing love and humanity is the greatest weapon to fight against everything that threatens the universe. All of them believed that the universe would find its own way and come out of the global pandemic any day sooner. Everything will be back to normal: the batch tour, the college farewell, Parties, Children playing in the park, reading books at the library, theatres, everything. Soon people will start hugging each other without any fear in their heart. After the pandemic, every kiss and hug would be even more valuable.

Nothing became normal as everybody expected. People started adapting themselves to the new reality. This pandemic taught everyone the value of love, families, mental health, personal hygiene, and a lot more. People started realising that "Nature is the only constant thing, and we are their guests". Love is the bridge which connects people in such difficult times.

Love is many things for people- happiness, security, sacrifice, strength. But in the global pandemic, love became a wireless network through which they communicate. It was also a test of their patience as they keep loving each other without sharing the physical closeness. They were eagerly waiting for the day when they get to see each other again. After six months, the lockdown was relaxed. Sarah and Karthik finally met each other in their favourite place. She hugged him as soon as he parked his bike and kissed him all over his face. They felt eternal love at that moment.

They were holding hands and started walking towards the beach. Sarah placed her head on his shoulder, and that was the moment she longed for the past six months. Without any gloves, masks, hand sanitizers, she felt safe around him. Later they bought coffee, and they had their coffee date again, after ages.

"I missed this!" Karthik told.

"Having Coffee with me or having coffee here?" Sarah asked.

"I actually like it when you interrupt me with your stupid questions, which is often, by the way. If our memories had to be associated with a distinct smell, it would be of coffee and this beach. You know, they say if you love something, you should set it free. You set me free like these waves, and you love me deeper like the sea. If I say, "I miss this", I mean "I miss us." You are aware of the coffee effect on me. But you're completely unaware of your effect on me." Karthik said and kissed her again. They spent the next three hours, sitting on the seashore and talking about his upcoming feature film. Our lives have changed so much in the past few months. Our routines have disappeared, rituals have fallen away. But the desire for true love has only gotten stronger. A lockdown and the global pandemic can be challenging, but love always finds its way.

"Finding true love in this time of quarantine and pandemic is what will give you lasting peace", Karthik wrote on his Facebook. Sarah commented, "And some Dalgona Coffee".

24

THIS ONE'S FOR YOU

by Jaya Prakash A

Is this what you do all day at school?" he plucked the notebook from my hands and threw it on the floor. I followed its trajectory and fell to my knees near where it fell. As I was about to pick it up, he kicked it away. Even a mere spot of ink at an unintended place on that notebook would have sent me down on a spiral of madness but right then it was being tossed away in the dirt: it broke my heart.

I followed it once again, and this time picked it up before he could reach it. Hugging it to the chest, I lied face down on the floor. I wanted to keep mom's precious notebook safe at all cost, even if it was all dirty by then. His fumbling hands couldn't find a way to reach it, so he retired himself to the living room with the muttering, "I am going to burn that thing one day."

As his footstep faded to silence, I got up and ran with the book still tucked near my heart to the kitchen. I breathed a sigh of relief as the presence of familiar things consoled me. Tears were struggling to be freed from my eyes when I reached for the single thing in the whole world, which had the power to make me feel better any moment: mom's pot of coffee. I put it on the stove, and as the coffee slowly warmed its way to a boil, my thoughts did the same.

The diary which dad had tried so hard to keep away from me was my mother's which I had found bundled up with some kitchen wares in the attic when I had been searching for a spare coffee cup. She had written only three pages on them. In those pages, she had talked about me, coffee, and her habit of writing. I felt her warm presence every time I hugged that diary to my chest and had been sleeping with it by my side every day since then. That notebook was the last piece of her left in my world, and I loved it as much as I could.

One day, I was lying on my bed with a cup of coffee next to me – I had wrapped a blanket around the cup to keep it secured on the uneven surface – and the diary was laid open before me. Till that moment, I had been thinking that it would be unthinkable to write on her notebook as it would mean sullying her memories. But I could never stop looking at its white pages as if there was something there to be understood; a puzzle which I thought if unlocked might tell me more about her.

But would that knowledge be safe? I remembered how dad had taken away everything about her except this one notebook and the coffee pot. If he could, he would burn that notebook too and then reach into my mind and erase every memory of her. That's when it struck me; these white pages were just blank, and all that was left of her was in my head, and if I were to forget, she would cease to exist for real that time. As panic ensued in my heart, my fingers gripped the pen and started writing everything I remembered about her with a desire to keep her alive forever in my words.

I began with my mornings. Every day since I could remember, I had woken up to the same things; the intoxicating smell of coffee, the whistle of a glass pot, and mom's face filled with anxiousness until she could take a sip from the freshly made coffee. Her beautiful face glimmering beyond the steam rising from coffee was what I badly wanted to wake up to.

Often, she would lie on her bed with the coffee cup sitting next to her with fragile balance and enthusiasm would sweep over her face as she would write on her notebook. I used to lie next to her in bed as she would kiss me and the coffee cup as much as she could while writing.

Those were the happiest days of my life, and then it vanished right before my eyes.

Mom had passed away in a tragic accident a few years before that, and soon after her death, father had come home, a military man who had been dismissed from the army out of disgrace because of his actions in the field, to live with me in a quiet little town in Tamil Nadu. After his arrival, mom's notebooks had started to disappear; I had thought he threw them all away. Soon, it felt as if she had never lived there.

Dad just stayed home for a long time. I had spent barely any time with him before mom's death, so I was confused about whether he was always like that. He wouldn't speak or do anything except eat; even that very rarely. He would buy meals and leave them outside my room without uttering a word.

Eventually, he was offered a job as a security guard in my school. My school principal was affectionate towards me because of my 'diligence and passion' as he would say, and when he heard that I lived in an uncomfortable situation, he offered my dad a job and waived my fee. But even after getting a job, dad remained almost the same, but the same couldn't be said for my mental health. Every day I lived with him, I felt that I was inching towards complete madness.

After finishing school, I got a degree in English from a local college with relative ease. All those years of writing countless diaries had sparked a deep interest in me for words, and my mind was slowly beginning to think what I might want to do in life with that interest.

A few months after graduating, I got a job offer in Bangalore. Not a job that I wanted but the fact that it was far away from home and cold, piercing eyes of dad made me so happy that I accepted without an ounce of thinking.

When I told him the news, he looked up at me, and our eyes met after so many years. I thought if only for a second, he would cry, hug, and beg me not to leave him, and say that if I left him, he would have nothing in his life. I didn't know what I would have done if he had done that, but I wanted to hear that. I had grown accustomed to his presence as cold as it was. But he left the room with a mere moan; he couldn't even bother to say a word of meaning. I felt assured that my decision to leave was correct.

Years passed; five whole numbers of them. One day on a lazy morning in March, I got a phone call from an unknown number while I was working from my cluttered desk at a local newspaper where I worked as an assistant editor. After all these years, I wouldn't have been surprised if I had forgotten his voice, but when he said hello, I knew it was him. It was dad, and he said he was waiting outside my room in Mumbai.

When I reached there hurrying with a mysterious care and curiosity dominating my mind, I saw him sitting on the floor next to the door with a small dirty leather bag. As I walked towards him, I took a clear look at him. At that sight, the strength in my knees vanished, and I almost buckled. It had been only five years, but he seemed to have aged at least thirty. His giant and broad frame which had menaced me through all of childhood had reduced to a frail and small structure.

His hair was white as snow, and his skin was sagging over his face; curving age lines covered his face like a fingerprint. He almost smiled when he saw me, but it disappeared quickly. He greeted me with a stern look, but his fragile appearance didn't feel cold as it had done before. Somehow, it was sad for the first time in my life.

We spent a few hours in silence in my room. Even though the air was feeling thicker and thicker as time passed, I didn't want to leave. I felt that it would be running away like how I did five years ago. Then suddenly he said, "You can go back to the office if you want." I almost chuckled and left remembering how cold he still is, and a part of me was scared to leave him there thinking that he might throw my notebooks and coffee cups away.

When I returned that night to my room, I was surprised to see the door was locked from outside. I stood there for a few minutes completely dumbfounded as to where he would have gone when the neighbour ran toward me and gave the key saying some old man gave it to him.

I went in, and the room was exactly as I left it was. I breathed a sigh of relief and sat on my bed. I noticed a coffee cup covered with a saucer was placed on my nightstand. It was filled with coffee, and the warmth had long left it; it must have been there for a while, and as I lifted it, I saw that there was a letter below it, and my heart suddenly began to race. I opened it.

It was written in shaky handwriting:

"Dear Sahana, I am not much of a talker, but my heart has grown too heavy to keep all these words inside anymore. What I say might not make sense or give you peace, but it's something I need to say.

When I heard that your mother died all those years ago, it changed me as a person, and eventually, it led me to being dismissed from my job. I don't regret losing it as I know I did not hurt anyone. But after losing the two of the things I loved most in the world, there was no going back to who I used to be.

At first, I tried to forget her because it was too painful to remember her knowing that I can never see her or hold her in my arms again. So, I put every little thing which reminded me about her away, but I couldn't do that to one thing. It was you. I saw your mother in your eyes, and that broke me every single time I looked at it. I thought I would get over it, but I never could.

I don't know if you remember this, but when you were studying in twelfth grade I grabbed and threw one of your mother's notebooks away from you because I was scared that you too would get stuck in life like me; unable to forget her.

I still can't accept that I have lost her: the love of my life, but I only realise now that I didn't need to lose you too. I...it's too late for everything, and I am sure you wouldn't want a dad who did nothing for you all through your life. I accept that. It's easier to accept because I can now feel assured that you are happy somewhere doing something you like. That's all I need; for you to be happy. I cannot expect you to forgive me for whatever I did or did not do, but I want to say I am sorry.

I have left a small leather bag in your room where I have put your mother's notebooks which I had kept hidden from you all these years. I am going back to home, and I won't disturb you ever again.

One last thing, I know you love coffee, so I made one for you. At least let this coffee be the one thing your father did for you in his life.

Dear Sahana, This one's for you."

I fell to the floor as tears flowed without control from my eyes. Years and years of pain which I had locked away carefully poured into my heart in an instant, and I felt paralysed. The letter was still tightly held in my hand as a decision began to form in my mind. I needed him there with me; there was no reason to lose another moment with him even if all of them were to be silent because he wasn't as bad as I thought him to be instead just broken like me.

I picked up my purse, and almost left the room when the cup on the nightstand caught my eye. Holding down the racing heart which was determined to reach him before he left Mumbai, I took a sip from the first coffee my dad had ever made for me, and once again tears fell out unceremoniously as I realised it's the best one I had ever tasted.

25

ONE LAST CUP

by C.L. Williams

Andrew makes his way to Jolt, his favourite coffee shop. It's the place where he met Mia. It's the place where he proposed to her as well. This is a day he wasn't expecting to happen. Jolt will now become the place where he says goodbye to Mia.

Andrew sits at the table, waiting for Mia when the barista makes her way to the table.

"Hi, Andrew." The barista says in a peppy voice.

"Hey, Anna," Andrew says in a sombre tone.

"I know everything," Anna says in an assuring tone as she places her hand on Andrew's shoulder. "That's why I wanted to tell you this order is on the house." Anna smiles before going back to her peppy self when she sees Mia walk through the door.

"Hi, Mia!" Anna says in excitement as she pulls out the chair for Mia.

"Hello, Anna," Mia says in a monotone voice. "Just get me the regular. Thank you." Mia smiles as Anna walks off. She then turns her attention to her former fiancé, Andrew.

"I hope you know, bringing me to the place where you proposed is not going to change things," Mia says, cutting to the chase.

"I never said I was trying to win you back. I told you I wanted to have a cup of coffee with you at Jolt. If my intentions were trying to rekindle what we once had, I would've made my intentions known." Andrew tells Mia.

"That's why we didn't work," Mia tells Andrew. "You have the weirdest of intentions, and you never make any sense. Who wants to have coffee with their former fiancé?" Mia asks.

"I'm not here to argue with you, and I'm not here to explain why I think we couldn't work as a couple. I asked you here so I could tell you what I wanted to say. Can I please say what I want to say?" Andrew asks.

Mia is silent, she nods and looks at Andrew, waiting for him to begin talking.

"I called meeting you here the best day of my life. I knew when I was ready to propose that this was the only place, I wanted that moment to happen." Andrew stops for a moment to breathe as he knows he is about to get emotional.

"When you told me you were carrying my child, *our child*, I looked to the skies, and I thanked God that very moment." Andrew gulps before finishing his words. He's about to resume his words, but Anna arrives at the table with two cups of hot coffee. Andrew has his black while Mia has her light roast with sugar and creamer.

"Here's the coffee," Anna says with a smile before walking off.

"Thanks, Anna," Andrew screams out before resuming his conversation with Mia.

"Please, continue," Mia tells Andrew.

"The moment you told me you lost the baby; I didn't know what to say. I didn't know how to act. I wanted to do everything I could to support you because I knew you here hurting in ways I didn't and still don't understand."

"What happened after that wasn't your fault." Mia does her best to assure Andrew he has nothing to be upset about.

"I know. That is why I asked you here." Andrew takes a sip of his coffee. "When I saw the note and your body on the floor when I got home, I felt my life was over." Andrew takes another sip of his coffee. "It took me this long to realise that I need to move on. I didn't ask you here for a reunion. I asked you here to get closure. I wanted one final cup of coffee with you. After that, I leave, and I move on with my life."

Mia pours the creamer in her coffee before taking a sip. "I understand. Can I ask of your future plans?" Mia asks.

"I think it's best if you don't." Andrew looks down at his coffee as he knows tears will fall from his face if he says those words to Mia's eyes. He soon looks up at her and says, "I hope wherever you are in the afterlife, you are receiving some mercy. You were a good person."

Mia smiles at Andrew and delivers a faint *Thank you*. Andrew looks up to say his final goodbye to his former fiancé, but she has already disappeared before he can say anything. He looks at the table, and he notices something. He sees a glimmer next to Mia's half-empty coffee cup. He moves Anna's coffee cup to the side, and the glimmer he was seeing came from the engagement ring he gave Mia. The night Andrew saw Mia unconscious, he didn't have it in him to remove the ring. He goes for it but pauses. He puts his hand back on his coffee cup and resumes sipping on his still hot coffee. While he is sipping on his coffee, Anna walks over to check on him.

"Are you okay, Andrew?" Anna asks.

"I will be. Thank you." Andrew says as he gives Anna a smile.

"It's just my nature to check on people."

"I didn't mean that." Andrew puts down his coffee. "I have been telling you for months that I wish I had better closure with Mia other than seeing a lifeless body in our bedroom. I don't know how you did it, but you helped give me the closure that I have been wanting for some time."

"It wasn't easy," Anna says. She places her hand on Andrew's shoulder, "If it helps if she were in a bad place, this meeting would have been impossible."

Andrew looks at Anna and smiles. "That does help more than you may know. While I needed the closure, I lost sleep many nights wondering if she were suffering wherever she maybe."

"Is there anything else I can do for you, Andrew?" Anna asks.

"Nothing else," Andrew says in an assuring tone. "Right now, I just want to finish this cup of coffee."

ACKNOWLEDGEMENTS

I'm incredibly grateful to everyone in Inkfeathers team for making this possible. I would like to thank and acknowledge all the writers who have given such beautiful and unique stories for the book. Special thanks to my sister- Shakthi and my best friends- Dhanshri, Durai and Jayaprakash for helping me right from the beginning, and for writing my Editor/author bio and also for giving me that strong push whenever I needed. To all my best friends who have cultivated the idea of publishing my own book and who have been dreaming about it more than me since I started writing, this is for all of you. Finally, and above all, thanks to my coffee. None of this would have happened without it.

MEET THE AUTHORS

S.C. Elliott

She is a typical creative who spends most of her day experiencing life, seeking the inspiration that compels her to write. She counts kayak excursions, candid conversation, and travelling the beautiful landscape of her native Florida as her three muses. When she isn't writing, she enjoys voice acting and singing.

Ida Williams

She works mostly in the misty days of historical fiction, sometimes wandering around Victorian London or listening to jazz in a 1950s New York café. She is currently creating short stories, online videos and is working on a novel.

Padmini Peteri

She is an avid reader who has a passion for writing her heart out. She writes short stories and poetry in both Hindi and English languages. To her, writing is healing and a way of expression. She mostly writes about mental health and social issues. She gets lost in the world of books, of imagination, of poems and stories. She believes in smiling and spreading happiness makes the world a better place to live in. Her writing finds wings in her Instagram handle @minithoughts_pp.

Harshita Garrepalli

She is a teen writer who often finds herself writing about the complexity of emotions and exhibits how vehemence can be expressed through paper. Along with writing relatable pieces, she also hopes to make all of her readers smile with her work. With myriad themes of love, friendship, betrayal, and writeups with blood on them, she hopes her writing can inspire and reach within the hearts of all those who rely on art for happiness.

Jaya Prakash A

There is no greater happiness in life than doing what you love. Jaya Prakash understands that, so he does it. He writes, runs, listens to music, plays, appreciates art, and cherishes relationships. He is no one unique; he is just a product of this world, but when he leaves it, the world will never be the same.

Shaymi Shah

She is a freelance architect by profession and a creative writer by passion. She was not a born writer but a cultivated one. Fascinated with her everyday world, she started writing insights on her daily observations, goaded by her own experiences. Time and again, she has attempted to find meaning in the simpler things, to find the beauty in the ordinary through her writing. Today, through a lot of practice, she has successfully imbibed in herself the skill of weaving stories- stories that one can easily lose themselves in. She believes that life is as natural as anything gets, and there's no way of really writing about it aptly with utmost detail- one just has to experience it and live in the moments.

Arati Harikumar

She is a passionate Human Resources professional working with Deloitte India. She relentlessly pursues many hobbies - a reader by day and writer by night, a dancer over the weekend and traveller when a destination beckons. She believes that there is so much to explore and experience in life, and one must never stop learning. A quote by Voltaire "Writing is the painting of the voice" sums up what she feels about writing - she is on a journey of finding her voice with every tale she spins.

Anshika Prem Chhatani

She is a budding Psychologist during the day and a stargazer for the night. She's also a Succeeding Graphologist and probably never misses a chance to dance! You'll always spot her with a book and coffee (well most of the times, if not always!)

Karan E

He is an altruist. As in a benevolent introvert who swoops in to help anyone and everyone no matter the consequences. He was neither a born writer nor a cultivated one. One day he picked up the pen and started writing what he saw around and what he felt. All-day, he listens to soul's and the stories they tell. He is a Mechatronics Engineer by day and Batman by night.

Krupa Prakruthi

She is a budding psychologist and the founder of Arista Psychological Support and Services. All her life, she has been a passionate advocate of mental health and is grateful to have found a career in the same. She envisions a world with no mental health stigma and affordable mental health care for everyone. She believes all animals deserve unconditional love and that kindness should be the primary human language.

Dr. Deepiga R

She is cute enough to stop your heart and skilled enough to bring it back. Doctor by profession, currently working in a rural hospital, she is well recognized for her excellent medical services. She is always fond of a world full of love, humanity, kindness and believes that love can heal everything. She has more love for coffee than anything, and the cafeteria is like a second home for her. Just a cup of coffee can make her do anything at any time. She loves to pen down her emotions than to share with people, also loves to write fantasy stories with happy endings.

Selvakumar Petchimuthu

He is a patriot, a soul that spreads without signs—the one who quenches the thirst caused by art with his own writings. He writes to numb the wandering souls. His words are like amla wine. He seeks to know the fragrance of flowers, the intense taste of fruits, and the mystery of nature. His life is like the last line of a story, beautiful yet complex.

Padmashri Jayaprakash

She is an adolescent kid-friendly with the sublime passion in writings. She is a joyful kid who enjoys being intrepid. She always holds a novel related to Human balance. Her biggest achievements are her seminars in her school days. She enjoys reading psychology-related books and articles. She is great in her words and scribbles. Her biggest strength is her words, and she firmly believes that words can even change an enemy into a good friend and also failures into success.

Archana Natarajan

She is a Bengaluru based blogger who likes to write in the romantic fiction and travelogue genres and is a regular contributor to StoryMirror and Indiblogger. She has also authored scientific articles as a Biochemist and is pursuing her PhD in Neurochemistry. Apart from blogging at http://aworldofcolors.blogspot.com and pursuing research, she also dabbles in candid wedding photography with her husband. Currently, she is busy juggling work and parenting responsibilities. She is also utilizing her creative juices in compiling interesting stories that she can share with her son as he is growing up.

Dheepan Ravikumar

He is not an engineer by profession but completed engineering. Not a professional writer but keeps writing. He is a listener, blogger, and content writer—an ordinary guy with infinite and uncensored dreams. Being an oblivion, he always loves to get himself lost with things that make him happier.

Karthick A

He is a neophyte-boffin who is curious to learn and understand the elegant universe. He is a blend of all kinds – an avid reader, a science zealot, an obsessive enthusiast, wanderlust, sapiosexual and an autodidact. He embraces both existentialism and nihilism. If you ask him what he thinks about himself, he whispers Rene Descartes' "Cogito Ergo Sum".

Peter Jewkes

In this life, he has had the following incarnations – baby, toddler, schoolboy, student, factory worker, railway worker, lecturer, professor, architect, space planner, chess player, restaurateur, maitre d', sommelier, painter, friend, husband, father, often quite a few at the same time. He is presently enjoying life with his beautiful family on a mountaintop in southern Spain.

Prerna Agrawal

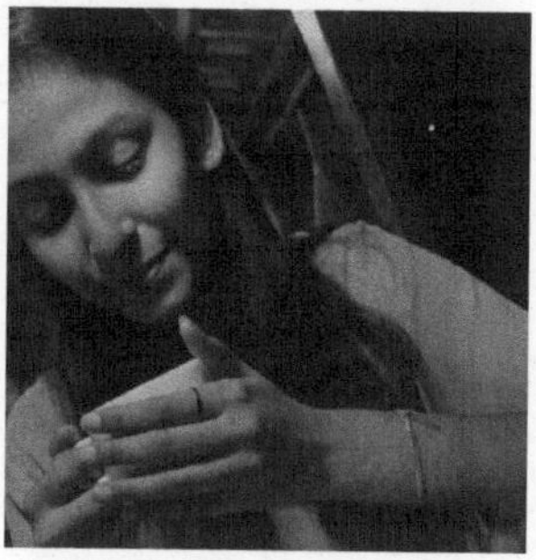

She is a girl for whom simplicity is the key to happiness. It wouldn't always be easy to do something, but she always tries to do what's right. She likes coffee as much as she likes herself: Sweet and strong. She believes that God has given us one life and we should not waste that on worrying about something or on those people for whom we don't mean anything, so we must live our life to the fullest and be such a person on whom people can look up to as an inspiration.

Suganya Kumar

Currently, she is pursuing her PhD. She is a huge fan of fantasy and dreams. She is not a professional writer; she just simply gives life to her thoughts and feelings. She is still learning and exploring the life of people around her. She considers her writing in this book is very special to her.

C.L. Williams

He is an international bestselling author living in central Virginia. He has written poetry, short stories, novellas, and one novel. C.L. Williams is currently putting the finishing touches on his poetry book OMNI- and Bed Bugs, the supplement book to the MMH Productions film of the same name.

OUR STORY

We're all on a Journey, and our "Writers" have made it Beautiful.

A dreamcatcher is an object made with feathers and strings, essentially used as lucky charms in many parts of the world. The same way, Inkfeathers brings together writers, editors, and artists together to form a dreamcatcher that works in favour for the young writers and readers and if you're positive about it, it may bring you luck as well.

We at Inkfeathers are connected to thousands of writers globally, who believe in the magic of telling stories. This stream of connectivity with the writers, the fact that everyone has a unique detail or edge to their story makes Inkfeathers proud to partner with these young literary as well as collaborative minds.

Back in 2013, our founders came together to form an offline group for their love of literature, and this formed collaborative energy with many young literature-wounded minds which eventually led these offline meetings to stand-ups, storytelling events, poetry slams, meet-ups to share experiences and many others. In 2016, Inkfeathers finally launched as the brand project under one Private Limited Company. This expanded opportunity gave a number of possibilities and a new way to expand our support for writers.

This dream of wanting to bring together writers as well as readers has come true beyond measure as writers connect to us from countries like the United States, United Kingdom, Canada each day to bring their stories to life.

As of this year, we are extremely delighted to provide you our website (www.inkfeathers.com) where all your queries can be resolved about our self-publishing process and latest anthologies. You can get hold of the latest updates on anthologies, events, offers, new book releases and so much more here. You can go ahead and order a book from our bookstore to get a taste of our mindful curation of stories and poems.

Inkfeathers Publishing family encourages you to really put your feelings out there in words for the world to see, in order to have a common ground to grow mutually. We are a creative platform for all those seeking literary help in terms of having their words published.

Believe us, publishing a book is not easy, but we come to a writer's rescue at each phase of having their book in print in terms of Editing, Designing, Branding, Marketing and all the other work that goes behind until you have a printed copy in your hands for Distribution. Together, it couldn't have been any easier. We will be there for you, to help you turn your manuscript into a freshly bound book that sells off the glass bookshelves.

With Love,
Inkfeathers Publishing